Murder in the Cemetery
An Edmund DeCleryk Mystery

By

Karen Shughart

For information, email Cozy Cat Press, cozycatpress@aol.com or visit our website at: www.cozycatpress.com

COZY CAT
P R E S S

ISBN: 978-1-946063-98-4
Printed in the United States of America

10 9 8 7 6 5 4 3 2 1

Dedication:

Lyle, my fabulous husband is, as always, my biggest champion, most honest critic and greatest fan. I love you dearly.

Patricia Rockwell, publisher extraordinaire, thanks for your support and confidence in me and for encouraging me to write the Edmund DeCleryk series.

Acknowledgements

Most of us have heard the expression, "It takes a village," and for me, an author of mysteries, the expression couldn't be more accurate. I simply could not be writing this series without the help of criminal justice and legal experts who have generously provided me with technical advice and answers to my many questions.

Their help with the first Edmund DeCleryk mystery, *Murder in the Museum,* made writing about investigative procedures and history in this book much easier. I'd be remiss in not thanking them again: Dave Phelps, Jason Maitland, Barry Virts, Jeffrey Fosdick, Steven Sklenar and the Sodus Bay Historical Society.

I couldn't have written *Murder in the Cemetery* without the help of Wayne County (NY) District Attorney, Michael Calarco, who was a terrific resource.

Our friend, Jim Quinn, a retired Rochester City policeman (and husband of my dear friend, Mary, one of my beta readers), helped me to understand that even in the toughest circumstances, a law-enforcement professional can be compassionate.

Sara Lichterman, media spokesperson for the CIA (yes, truly, the CIA!) provided me with information about the organization and correct terminology to use when describing personnel. Because this is a work of fiction, Ed's interviews with employees of that Agency and other details may not always be accurate. I take full responsibility for errors.

My beta readers: husband Lyle; daughter Jessica Hurwitz; and dear friends Mary Quinn; Shelley Usiatynski and Deb Vater have provided constructive criticism and lots of good suggestions. To Alice Bill, you know why.

I borrowed the term, ROMEOs, from Aaron Hurwitz. If you aren't familiar with the acronym, you'll learn what it means in chapter five.

The recipe for Ellie's Beans was given to me by my friend, Ellen Warren, who passed away several years ago after an incredibly courageous fight against cancer. I miss you, dear friend, and hope readers of this book will enjoy preparing and tasting this delicious crock-pot side-dish.

Last, but not least, I want to thank my family. You have all been promoters and champions: Lyle (of course), Jessica (again), Jeremy Hurwitz and our daughter-in-law, Debbie Bux-Hurwitz; my siblings Alan Green, David Green and Marcy Brody and their spouses/significant others.

PROLOGUE ONE
September 1814- Lighthouse Cove, NY

Standing in the yard of her sprawling, blue-shuttered, yellow frame house, Rebecca Fitzhugh could see Silver Bay, and beyond it, Lake Ontario. From the east, a flotilla of British warships, sails unfurled, plowed through the turbulent waters toward the harbor. She was prepared.

Six years earlier, her beloved husband Robert had emigrated from England to work with his cousin, Morgan Lewis, a former state governor and now Quartermaster General for Western New York. He had been assigned to a post near Lighthouse Cove and several months later, after meeting at a church supper, he and Rebecca had married.

Now a patriot, Robert had become increasingly alarmed at reports that the ships were heading toward their village for provisioning and to wage battle. He'd quickly organized a ragtag militia to repel the invaders.

Rebecca felt sympathy for her husband, understanding full well that with family still residing in England, his loyalties must be divided. Nevertheless, he had taken an oath of allegiance to his adopted country, and an honorable man, had pledged to help protect it.

After receiving a message from Cousin Morgan that the war ships were making headway despite ferocious winds and waves cresting at fifteen feet, the couple developed a plan to assure Rebecca's safety and that of their daughters. The day was warm for September, but still, she shivered with trepidation.

"Children," she called out to her two sweet girls, ages three and four, who were playing in the garden with their cat, Nicely, "You must come into the house immediately, and please bring kitty."

Patience, the four-year-old, looked at her mother, stamped one foot and whined, *"Not coming*, mama. I want to stay outside."

Her sister, Charity, nodding in agreement, announced with confident authority, "Mama, I *will* stay outside." Then she remembered her manners. "Please, may I?"

Amused at their assertiveness and exasperated at the same time, Rebecca quickly realized the children couldn't possibly understand what lay ahead. She must remain calm.

"We're going on a journey, just a short one, to visit your Aunt Marigold and Uncle Remington. Quickly now, we must leave today. You can bring Nicely and your dollies."

The little girls jumped up and down with pleasure. "Auntie and Uncle, yes, let's visit them!" Patience yelled.

Rebecca smiled. Her sister and brother-in-law owned fifty acres of land where they grew apples, several miles south of the lake and in no danger from British invasion. She would take the carriage and as many belongings as she could carry. She had not seen her husband for two days, prayed their separation would be brief, and that when she returned to the village, he would be alive and their home among those left unharmed.

PROLOGUE TWO
This Century
Lighthouse Cove, NY

It was the first of May, and the day awoke with a brilliant sun that cast its rose gold rays over Lake Ontario and Silver Bay, eliciting diamond-like shards of light that danced through the waves, surprising the foraging gulls with their brilliance.

The winter had ended and then, in April, the winds had roared in from the north and the rains came in blinding, unrelenting torrents, shaming typhoons and hurricanes with their fierceness. The angry sea, having no choice, coughed up cascades of turbulent water that crashed over seawalls, lured docks away from their moorings, and flooded already overburdened pumping stations. With not a whimper, but a bang, it ended as abruptly as it had begun.

Spring in Lighthouse Cove overshadowed its neighbors to the south. In the south, spring came gradually, like a cloud gently, slowly, obscuring the sun. First, the snowdrops, then the crocuses, then the daffodils and tulips. In the north, on the lake, in Lighthouse Cove after the rains stopped, spring arrived in splendiferous glory—all manner of flora blooming at once—inciting a riot of color: pale pink, mauve, bright yellow, resplendent red, innocent white, luscious purple.

Today, this first day of May, as residents of Lighthouse Cove awoke to a brilliant sun that cast its rose gold rays over the water, they couldn't help but appreciate that they'd survived the harsh winter and that spring had finally and gloriously arrived.

SPRING
Chapter 1

Annie DeCleryk, executive director of the Lighthouse Cove Museum and Historical Society, hadn't planned to wake up just after the break of dawn, but her eleven-year-old beagle, Gretchen, jumped on the bed, nudged her face with her nose and then, annoyed when Annie didn't immediately respond, pounced on top of her. Gretchen needed to go out. Correction: Gretchen, desperate to go out, knew that once back inside she'd get breakfast, and eating was at the top of the list of best things for beagles; walks and snuggles, second and third.

Ed, Annie's husband, normally awoke early to let the dog out, but the retired police chief turned criminal consultant had been in Watertown for two days working on a project with the police force there and wouldn't be home until evening. With a groan, Annie stretched and got out of bed, walked downstairs in her nightgown and almost tripped over the dog who was flipping and jumping at her feet.

She opened the back door, which led from the spacious kitchen of the old ship captain's home, to a wide wraparound porch and expansive yard that faced the lake. Despite the early hour, she could see two small sail boats bobbing about, and in the distance, a fishing trawler.

Gretchen trotted out, did her business quickly, and then scratched at the door to come back inside. After Annie let her in, she ran at break-neck speed to the closet where her food was stored. Yawning, Annie measured half-a-cup, put it in her bowl and set it on the floor with another bowl containing fresh water. The dog finished eating in ten seconds, licked the bowl for any remaining specks and crumbs for another ten then took a huge drink.

Now fully awake, the petite, blue-eyed woman with short, tousled gray hair realized with a delighted start that the rain that had bombarded the village for weeks had ended, and the day had dawned bright and clean. She walked outside. The luminous sun shone over the water; the birds were singing their morning songs. Contrails of white, orange and pink streaked the vivid blue sky. For the first time since late fall, she could smell the fresh, verdant scent of the lake.

She had planned to go into work early; then reconsidered. The museum was in fine shape for its formal opening on Mother's Day weekend. The gift shop had been stocked, the docents trained, and she had hired an intern, Jason Shipley, a twenty-year-old communications' major at Rochester Institute of Technology, to write brochures for her on the history of Lighthouse Cove.

Jason had completed the first, on the Revolutionary War, ahead of schedule and had just begun to research the War of 1812. Annie had suggested he interview her friend, Amanda Reynolds, a retired teacher, historian and biographer. He'd promised to call her that morning; then visit the old cemetery where patriots, who had died protecting Lighthouse Cove during that war, were buried.

He might want to wait a while before visiting the cemetery, Annie had cautioned him. In an extreme state of disrepair, it had not been maintained for years because of budgetary constraints. Circumstances changed after a $500,000 endowment to the museum from the estate of deceased board member, Emily Bradford, had provided funds that would allow the project to begin this summer. Ever curious and not easily deterred, the intern responded that a derelict cemetery might reveal far more than a perfectly intact and manicured one.

Yes, Annie had second thoughts, not only about going into work early, but about going into work at all. She wanted to dig in the garden. She wanted to begin spring cleaning. She wanted to sit in the sun. And, she wanted to take Gretchen for a long walk to the beach and along the bluff that overlooked the lake.

Jason was expected at the museum at 9:00. She'd call and ask him to retrieve the mail and put a sign on the door that the museum would be closed until tomorrow. After meeting with Amanda and visiting the cemetery, he could go home. Spring was finally here, and the day much too lovely to spend inside a dark, musty old building.

Chapter 2

A few blocks away, Annie and Ed's friends, George and Sally Wright, had also awakened early. While Sally went into the kitchen to prepare their coffee, George, in sleeping pants and a tee-shirt, opened the French doors leading to their screened-in porch that overlooked Silver Bay.

"Looks like it's going to be a beautiful day," he remarked as Sally brought two steaming cups of coffee and three Morning Glory muffins that George had baked the night before—one for her, two for him—out to the porch on a tray. George, a tall, trim man with an unruly shock of iron gray hair that matched his eyes, took the tray from Sally and laid it on a small, round lime-green metal table that had been placed between two white Adirondack-styled rocking chairs.

"It certainly does," responded Sally, a slight, blond woman with warm, hazel eyes, as she watched a flock of sea gulls dive bomb into the bay, searching for food.

George and Sally had both grown up in Rochester, but George had spent his summers in Lighthouse Cove at Windy Bluff, his family's ancestral home that dated back to the mid-1800s.

A former Navy SEAL, George had left the service after 20 years and became a teaching fellow at Boston College where he obtained a masters' degree in international finance. After receiving his degree, he was hired as a financial services advisor at Barrow and Croft, a firm in Rochester; he'd retired several months earlier. He and Sally sold their home in the city and moved into Windy Bluff after his parents, elderly and with deteriorating health, purchased a smaller, one story cottage a few blocks away.

Sally walked back into the kitchen to get a second cup of coffee when the phone rang. She recognized the caller ID and answered.

"Hi, Lily."

The caller was the Wright's daughter, Lily Klein, who worked from home as a graphic designer and lived in Brighton with her husband, Eric, a history professor at the University of Rochester, and their two young children.

"Hi, Mom."

"How nice to hear your voice, but it's awfully early. Everything okay?"

"Yes. I've decided I'm not working today. Would you like to go to Skaneateles with me? I want to do some shopping and enjoy the lovely weather. If you can join me, I'll pick you up around 9:30."

"What about the children?" Sally asked.

"We've got it covered, Mom. Eric has no classes today."

"Then I'd like to go with you, but first let me make sure your father doesn't have plans for us." Sally held the phone away from her ear and called to George, "We don't have any commitments today, do we? Lily's invited me to go to Skaneateles with her."

George walked into the kitchen and replied, "No specific plans." He grinned. "But please tell her I'm disappointed she hasn't invited me to come along. It's been ages since she and I have spent any quality time together."

"Did you hear him, Lily? Your father's giving you a hard time."

Lily laughed. "I did. Tell him this is a mother-daughter day out. I promise I'll call him soon and invite him to lunch."

"Why don't you talk to him yourself? Here, George. Your daughter wants to speak with you."

After a conversation that lasted about three minutes, George handed the phone back to Sally. She and Lily spoke for a few minutes more and then ended the call.

"What are you and Lily planning to do in Skaneateles?" George asked his wife, his eyes sparkling.

"Lily wants to go to La Maison to purchase some napkins and placemats, then to the vinegar and oil store. We'll have lunch on the porch at the Nottingham Inn, and she's going to try and make a reservation for pedicures at Spa Papillion."

"Sounds like a busy day. Will you have time to get some cookies for me at the Village Bakery?"

"I'll make time," Sally responded with a smile. "What kind do you want?

"How about double chocolate chip and some oatmeal, walnut and raisin?"

"I'll buy a half dozen of each. What's on your agenda?"

"It's much too pleasant to stay indoors, I'm going to take a long walk this morning; after that, work on repairing our dock and, depending on how long that takes, try and get the boat into the water. My Navy buddies are meeting for lunch at noon at Phillips House. I said I'd join them, but I don't want to be bogged down by commitments, so I told Bob Fergus when we spoke yesterday that I'd call and let him know if my plans change. What time will you be home?"

"Probably by late afternoon."

"Do you want me to fix anything for dinner, or would you rather go out?"

"You know I can't say no to the fabulous desserts at the Inn. Instead of eating here, let's go to The Brewery. You can get a full meal, and I can get a salad or appetizer if I'm not that hungry."

"Sounds like a plan," George replied.

Chapter 3

After waving goodbye to his wife and daughter at
9:30, George, now dressed in jeans, a tee shirt and
sturdy hiking shoes, began his walk, starting out toward
the beach, which lay at the tip of a small peninsula
where a channel from the lake cut into the bayside
harbor.

Today even the birds were pleased with the change
in the weather and joyfully formed a chorus for their
own pleasure and the villagers' delight. George could
identify the chirring of the robins, mournful cooing of
the doves, rancorous cawing of crows, and the mixed
melodies of sparrows, wrens, and cardinals.

Charming, old summer cottages that had been passed
down in families for generations lined both sides of the
road, those on the north facing the lake, and on the
south, the bay. During the winter, the floating docks
bayside had been moved onto land and securely placed
top to bottom against each cottage. Now, most of them
had been moved back into the water, and a few boats
were moored against them.

Feeling peaceful and relaxed, George stood for a few
minutes and watched the teal blue lake nudge perky
whitecaps onto the beach in front of the now closed
snack bar, the Gull Shack, which, in a couple of weeks,
would be serving tall cones of locally-made ice cream,
sandwiches of fried lake perch; salt potatoes, a local
favorite, and a variety of beverages.

A tall, towered lighthouse with a red lantern housing
its Fresnel lens blinked at passing ships at the end of the

200-foot pier that jutted out into the lake. Fishermen, taking advantage of the temperate weather, cast their lines into the water as gulls dive-bombed for their bait.

After leaving the beach, George made a right turn from Bay Street onto Lake View Road where historic homes built on a bluff more than 150 years ago stood, their yards rimmed with hedges of bright yellow forsythia and clusters of spring flowers.

Within a few minutes, he reached a gravel hiking trail that skirted the bluff. He had walked that trail many times as a boy but for some reason had never explored the dirt path at the end of it that meandered into the woods.

George tentatively tested the ground with one foot. Riddled with stones and rocks, it held firm, and he decided to continue walking, curious to see where the path led. He had hiked for about five minutes before spotting a small clearing, partially overgrown with weeds. Walking through the underbrush, he discovered what appeared to be an old, untended cemetery.

At its entrance, he tore dead vines away from a large concrete obelisk sticking out of the ground, a memorial to patriots who'd been killed during the War of 1812, after British invaders burned down most of the village.

I had no idea this was here, thought George.

Pervasive decay and rot had spread tentacles throughout the cemetery. Uprooted grass lay in disordered clumps, headstones had been tossed, helter-skelter, and the mud, plundered from the thieving water and wind, covered the site with a thick layer of sludge.

Those who had died in that war had been buried quickly in shallow graves, many in simple shrouds or hastily constructed pine boxes. The recent storm had coughed up bits and pieces of shredded muslin and slivers of rotted wood. George, appalled, spied what appeared to be some bones scattered about.

Surely Annie must know about the deplorable condition of this site, George thought, but, unaware of the museum's recent endowment, acknowledged that even if she did, finding funding to restore it might be challenging.

He expected Annie wouldn't mind if he got some volunteers to clean up the cemetery, repair the damaged grave sites and provide ongoing maintenance. Sally and some of her garden club friends might want to help, maybe some of his Navy buddies would also be interested.

He'd walk home to get tools, trash bags and his truck. Then, after spending the rest of the morning cleaning up some of the debris, he'd head over to the restaurant at lunchtime to pitch the project to his friends. He decided to postpone working on the dock until after lunch, and then, time permitting, he'd get the boat in the water before Sally came home.

A stream of sunlight snaked its way through the dense thicket of trees that stood along the bluff and landed on an object sticking up from the mud that caught George's eye. He picked it up and had begun to clean it with the hem of his shirt when he was startled by a noise in the woods behind him. As he turned towards the sound, he noticed a flash of rust and assumed it was a vixen and her kits hunting for food.

He finished cleaning the object, and excited about his discovery, placed it in his jeans pocket and walked to the path. Back on the trail, he pulled out his cell phone and dialed the number of the historical society, hoping to speak with Annie. The machine beeped. He left a lengthy message, requesting that she get back to him soon as possible.

Chapter 4

Amanda Reynolds didn't wake up to see the sunrise because she'd overslept. She'd watched an old movie on TV the night before and hadn't gotten to bed until after 1:00 a.m. The phone on her nightstand rang at 9:45, jarring her awake. She answered the call, and after a pleasant five-minute conversation, hung up the phone and gingerly slid out of bed; her arthritic hip bothered her the most, first thing in the morning. The 85-year-old rarely complained; she was grateful to be alive and relatively healthy for her age.

She looked out her bedroom window. The sun shone brightly for the first time in weeks. *Thank the Lord, no more rain,* she thought. In fact, it was a glorious morning, and she happily anticipated being able to spend part, or most of the day, outside in her garden supervising the nice man she'd hired to help her with yard work after her arthritis had worsened. He'd remove the branches and leaves that had peppered the yard from the storm, fertilize the early bloomers and prune the dead wood from those that would blossom later in the season. That would be after she met with her young visitor, who was expected later that morning.

After completing a few simple stretches to limber up, she went into the bathroom to take a shower then, dressed in casual black slacks and floral printed blouse, mixed up a batter of currant scones, placed them in the oven to bake, retrieved a jar of homemade lemon curd from her pantry and plugged in the electric kettle to heat the water for tea.

She set a small table in the sunroom, her favorite place this time of year, with a lovely patterned cloth and napkins, two small English bone china tea pots, and two matching cups and plates that had been passed down through generations in her family. A variety of herbs, planted towards the end of winter, sat in small containers on the windowsills. Those dried from last year's harvest sat labeled in small glass jars on shelves against one wall along with small cobalt blue bottles containing homemade tinctures of lavender, lemon balm, coneflower and mint, among others.

The charming home had been built by her ancestor, Robert Fitzhugh, in the 19th century but had changed hands many times since then and eventually fallen into disrepair. She and her late husband, Ernest, had purchased and lovingly restored it, delighted it was finally back in her family. Set high on a hill, it had views of the bay and beyond it, the lake, and collected refreshing lake breezes.

Her dearest friend, Eleanor Brown, members of her church and Annie DeCleryk were among her closest companions, others had moved away or were deceased. She and Ernest had been childless, and her neighbors on either side, couples with small children, were polite and friendly but much too busy with their own lives to pay attention to her.

She no longer drove and had sold her car; now her friends transported her to the market for food shopping and to doctors' appointments and social engagements. After they brought her home, they frequently didn't linger. Her visitor would be a welcome respite from the tedium of living alone.

Along with gardening, Amanda had once enjoyed leading-lady status while performing with a local summer repertory group; now most of the plays had few parts for women of her age. Her other passion was writing. She had authored some articles and books on the history of Lighthouse Cove that were available at the historical society, county libraries, gift shops and bookstores. She was, she admitted to herself, a local celebrity.

Writing, as with everything else that required dexterity, was becoming increasingly more difficult. Her fingers continued to stiffen, and after an hour or two at the computer, her hips, back and knees hurt. She didn't like relying on painkillers; herbal remedies seemed to work, at least for a few hours.

She had just put the tea leaves in each of the pots and poured in the boiling water when the doorbell chimed. Her visitor had arrived, and she was so looking forward to their conversation.

Chapter 5

A few minutes before noon that same day, a small group of retired Navy SEALs, they called themselves the ROMEOs—Retired Old Men Eating Out—met at Phillips House, their usual hangout located high on a hill overlooking hundreds of acres of apple orchards. The mild winter and recent rains had caused the trees to bloom earlier than expected, and their blossoms gave off a sweet, cotton candy scent.

The restaurant had been remodeled and expanded over the winter with new paint and modern furniture supplanting the cozy but dated decor from the 1970s. Instead of entering a foyer with a large dining room beyond it, patrons now entered directly into a room with a long, curved mahogany bar. The dining room had been replaced with two new ones built to the left and right of the bar, one facing north towards the lake, and the other, south. The focal point of each was a fireplace with a brick hearth and an elaborate brass and crystal chandelier. Round oak tables with cast iron pedestals had been set for lunch with black linen place mats and a colorful array of cloth napkins.

The sun was warm, and the men chose to sit outside on the north-facing deck, where the owners had hastily retrieved tables, chairs and umbrellas from winter storage. The tops of the apple trees with their profusion of white blossoms formed a lush carpet beneath them. Beyond, far in the distance, they could see the lake and white caps rolling toward the shore.

Within minutes, the friends were quickly served their beverages—two of them ordered coffee; one of them, beer—then they sat quietly as they perused their menus. Each had decided on the daily special, a roast beef club with choice of slaw or fries, and a pickle. Before the server returned to take their orders, Larry Mandel asked whether the other two members of their group would be joining them.

"Ed's not going to be here," Jeff Ketchum replied. "He's consulting on a project for the police force in Watertown and won't be back until this evening."

"What about George? Has anyone heard from him?" Larry asked.

"I spoke with him yesterday," Bob Fergus answered. "He said if the rain stopped, he wanted to spend the day repairing his dock and getting the boat in the water; still, he thought he'd be able break for lunch and join us. He promised to let me know if his plans changed."

"He could be on his way and is just running late. Maybe we should wait to order our food until he gets here," Larry suggested.

"I'll call him, just to make sure he's coming." Bob retrieved his cell phone from his pocket. After several rings, George's message line picked up.

"Hey, buddy, it's Bob. We're at the restaurant. If you get this message within the next few minutes call and give me an update of your status."

He looked at his friends. "If he's out on his dock, he may not have his phone with him and might have lost track of time, or he could be having a senior moment and forgot. We're all entitled to an occasional one at our ages."

The others laughed. He continued, "I guess we should go ahead and order without him."

Chapter 6

Annie spent most of the morning dusting books and
polishing furniture in the living room, ate a light lunch
at 12:30, then decided she'd done enough house
cleaning and picked up the phone to make calls she'd
been putting off.

She scheduled dentist and eye doctor appointments.
She spoke with the public affairs coordinator at the
hospital where she volunteered one Sunday a month, to
let her know she'd attend the annual tea. After that, she
called the local nursery to ask whether the purple
petunias, herbs, Gerbera daisies and tomato plants were
in stock.

Now, she was ready to be outside enjoying the
balmy weather. She called her friend, Suzanne Gordon,
hoping she'd be able to walk to the beach with her and
Gretchen that afternoon. Suzanne, who as a child had
emigrated with her family from the Caribbean island of
Jamaica to Rochester, ran the wellness center in the
village and served as the museum's board president.

Despite an almost twenty-year difference in their
ages, the two had bonded when Ed had investigated the
horrific murder of their friend, Emily Bradford.
Suzanne responded she'd love to join Annie, but she
couldn't leave until after her last yoga class ended at
3:00.

"I can wait. I'll run some errands and do some
gardening. Ed's in Watertown on business and won't be
back until 8:00 or later. I'd love to have company for

dinner, will you join me? We can have a glass of wine on the porch, and I'll fix something simple."

"That would be delightful," Suzanne replied, a melodious lilt to her voice. "We haven't spent much one-on-one time together lately, and I'm looking forward to catching up. I'll close the center and come and get you by 3:30."

Over the winter, Annie and Ed had constructed a wine cellar in their basement. She went downstairs and picked out a bottle of crisp Pinot Grigio that would accompany that evening's meal and placed it in the refrigerator to chill.

A few minutes later, Annie got into her car to drive to the market to purchase salmon, tomatoes and fennel for dinner that evening along with mixed greens for a salad and a loaf of crusty whole grain bread. The museum was on her way; she decided to stop and check for phone messages and open the mail Jason said he'd place on her desk.

His car was in the parking lot. When they'd spoken a few hours earlier, he'd indicated that after meeting with Amanda and before going home, he planned to go back to the museum to write some notes. She called out to him. When he didn't answer, she figured he hadn't heard her. She climbed the steps to his office, not wanting to startle him. He wasn't there; she assumed he'd walked to the meeting, and it was taking longer than expected.

As she turned to leave, she noticed an amber-colored plastic prescription container with a white cap sitting on his desk. She knew she was snooping, but curious, picked it up. Jason's name was on it. When she read the label, she became concerned. It appeared he was being treated for a serious medical condition; she hoped at some point he'd feel comfortable confiding in her about it.

Going back downstairs, she went through the mail, most of it junk that she tossed, then listened to her voice mail. George Wright had left an intriguing message; curious, she called him back. When he didn't answer, she decided to drive over to Lake View Road, hoping he was still at the cemetery.

Annie recognized George's red pickup truck parked in a space at the end of the trail. She parked next to it and got out of her car. Despite the rain, the path that led to the burial grounds wasn't terribly muddy, but it was strewn with rocks and pebbles, and she was wearing sandals. She decided she could meet with him some other time.

She got into her car and started to drive away when she had an idea. She dialed George's number again. This time when he didn't answer, she left a message requesting that he meet her at the site between 3:45 and 4:00 and to call if the timing wasn't going to work. She drove to the market, and after she returned home, called Suzanne.

"Silver Bay Wellness Center, this is Suzanne," her friend answered.

"Hi, Suzanne, it's Annie. Are you able to talk?"

"I have a couple minutes before my next class starts. What's up?"

Annie told her friend about the message she'd received from George Wright and summarized the sequence of events that followed it.

"I'd like to change plans and instead of walking to the beach, walk to the cemetery. George hasn't called back to reschedule, so I'm assuming the meeting is still on."

"That's fine with me, Annie."

"Bring sturdy shoes. We're going to have to tromp through the woods."

"I don't have any here at the center. I'll need to run home after the class ends and get them. It will only take a few minutes. See you later."

Chapter 7

Suzanne arrived at Annie's house a few minutes after 3:30. The two friends hugged, and then with Gretchen in tow, headed out the door.

The women were quiet for a few minutes as Gretchen sniffed, explored and relieved herself. Then Annie said, "The cemetery is in awful shape; if you've not been there, you're going to be very distressed when you see it."

"I'm embarrassed to admit I haven't," Suzanne replied. "I'm glad George is interested in helping to restore it. We'll have to let him know we have the money from Emily's estate and can hire some experts to assist him."

Annie replied that she'd already started making inquiries, and she expected George would be pleased to have the support. Still, now that he was retired, he had plenty of time to work on the project.

Changing the subject, she asked, "Suzanne, have you met my friend, Amanda Reynolds?"

Suzanne nodded. "Yes, I have, briefly at one of the museum's Christmas parties. Isn't she an author and historian?"

"She is. She wrote a wonderful biography about her ancestor, Robert Fitzhugh, the patriot who became a hero of the War of 1812. He formed a militia to repel the British and helped save some of the homes in the village from burning. Most of the militia died during the battle; he and two others who'd survived were captured and taken on board one of the ships. They supposedly didn't have enough room on board for all three and released two of them in Sackets Harbor on their way toward the St. Lawrence River. Robert wasn't one of them."

Annie continued, "He'd been a British subject before emigrating to the states and was transported back to England. According to Amanda's book, he was tried there for treason and hanged. His wife, Rebecca, who was born in New York, traveled to England with their two small daughters to be with him during the trial and hanging."

"How terribly sad," Suzanne responded. "I'm a little sketchy about the details of that war, but didn't it end when the two countries signed some sort of peace treaty?"

"Yes, the Treaty of Ghent, and that happened shortly after Fitzhugh reached England. I imagine it's also why his family was able to safely make the trip across the ocean."

Suzanne asked, "Given the timing of the treaty, doesn't it seem strange to you that our government, in appreciation for his heroism, didn't negotiate for his release?"

"Maybe signals got crossed. Remember, communication wasn't as fast as it is today, letters would have been transported between the two countries by ship. I'm speculating, but if the U. S. did send a letter with an emissary, perhaps by the time it reached King George, III it was too late."

"That's tragic. What happened to his wife and children?"

"Robert's parents, members of British nobility, took Rebecca and her daughters in after he died. She never returned to the states. It's rumored that she and her sister, who lived in Pennington, corresponded regularly, and that her sister saved all the letters. The letters have never been found."

"That's unfortunate. They'd probably shed some light on Rebecca's state of mind during her voyage to England and after her husband died," Suzanne remarked.

Annie nodded. "Amanda's book is fascinating. We have it in the library; would you like to read it?

"I would. I'll borrow it next time I'm in the building," Suzanne promised. "Speaking of projects, how's Jason working out?"

"I'm very pleased with him. He's making good progress writing the historical brochures about our village that tourists have requested; in fact, he's already completed the one on the Revolutionary War and is just beginning his research on the War of 1812. He called Amanda this morning and scheduled an interview with her. She'll be an excellent resource for him."

"After he's finished with this one, what's next?"

"The next one will be about Lighthouse Cove's involvement with the underground railroad before and during the Civil War; then he'll write one on rum running during Prohibition, and after that, the POW camp in Elmwood Park during World War II."

"That certainly takes pressure off you."

"It does, and I'm grateful I can afford to pay him. His being with us is freeing me to do other things I've put on hold at the museum." She linked arms with Suzanne. "And also, to take long walks with you, my dear friend."

From the Letters of Rebecca Fitzhugh
September,1815

My dear sister, Marigold,

The trip from Lighthouse Cove to the St. Lawrence River was arduous, but the weather held, and our first stop in Sackets Harbor for provisioning met with no untoward incidents, now that we are on peaceable terms with the British.

I write this from Ile de Montreal, where we have stopped again, as our store of food and supplies is getting low, and the next leg of our journey will be a long one. The settlers have been welcoming, and because our beloved tutor taught us all manner of things when we were young, I have been able to communicate with these gracious French speaking people.

The crew is quite taken with Nicely, who has turned out to be quite the mouser, and with my dear girls, who see this as a grand adventure. They do not, praise God, understand the significance of this trip and believe that we will soon be permanently reunited with their beloved father. I have not the heart to disabuse them of this. We are in good health.

Our ship's captain, Mr. Pengelley, has assured me that his seaworthy schooner can withstand the strongest of storms, but we should have smooth sailing to the next port of call, Newfoundland. He tells me that snow falls earlier there than in Lighthouse Cove, and the North Atlantic will be too rough for safe travel. We will spend our winter in St. Johns, with him and his wife. I will write to you then. Come spring, we should be able to continue our journey and reach our destination by early summer.

I do miss my dear Robert and fear that he will have been tried and hanged for treason before we disembark at the Port of London. I have written to his parents and ask that they inform him of our journey and send news of him to the captain's address in Newfoundland. I am distressed to think it will be months until I receive their response and by then he may be in our Lord's hands.

I trust you and Remington are well, that the apple harvest will be abundant, and you are enjoying what is always a beautiful late summer along the lake.

With love and affection, your sister,
Rebecca

Chapter 8

George's truck was parked at the end of Lake View Road. Annie held tightly onto Gretchen's leash as she and Suzanne walked down the rocky path towards the cemetery, pleased they'd worn sturdy hiking shoes. As they neared their destination, the beagle, head low to the ground, began sniffing, and the fur rose along the length of her back. She emitted a throaty growl and started running, pulling Annie, who struggled to control her.

They reached the cemetery, and Gretchen tugged hard, causing her leash to snap off her collar. In horror, Annie watched as she ran towards the bluff, terrified she was on a scent and would end up going over the precipice in pursuit. Then, abruptly, she slowed down, and Annie realized why her pet was so agitated.

A man lay face down in the mud. His right hand was stretched out in front of him, clutching a cell phone. Beside him lay a paper to-go cup, dark liquid spilled around it. Frantic, the dog began to bay as she clawed through the mud to his body. Annie's heart sank. She had a feeling she knew who it was.

The two women rushed over to him. His head was turned to the right and beside it, a pool of vomit. His body was stiff, in the first stages of rigor mortis; the women were unable to turn him onto his back. They noticed that his lips were blue; his face pulled into a deadly grimace. He had some sort of rash on his face and arms. Annie gasped. There was no mistaking George Wright, and he was dead.

Annie's hands were shaking, and she could barely speak. She managed to whisper, "I'll call 911, but we'll need to get back to the road. The cell phone reception is terrible here."

Suzanne asked, "Do you think he had a heart attack?"

Annie shrugged. "I have no idea, and I've learned through Ed to never jump to conclusions. Mike Garfield, our medical examiner, will determine the cause of death." She felt dizzy and queasy, too, and took several deep breaths to steady herself. After several seconds the nausea abated.

Gretchen was running in circles and whining; Annie sternly commanded her to sit while she put the leash back on her and then walked with Suzanne to the road. She placed the call, telling the dispatcher she and her friend would remain by George's truck until Mike and the emergency personnel arrived; then, escort them to his body.

"George and Ed were friends, weren't they?" Suzanne asked after Annie ended the call.

Annie nodded. "Yes, from childhood. And his wife, Sally, has become a dear friend of mine. She'll be devastated."

"Are you going to call Ed?"

"He's probably still in a training session, and he'll have a long drive back here from Watertown after a long day. I don't want him to be distracted. As sad and upset as I am, I'll wait until he gets home to give him the horrible news."

Gretchen continued to sniff and pull, and Annie was losing patience. She asked Suzanne if she would take her home and, when her friend agreed, pulled a door key out of her pocket and handed it to her.

"You don't know how long you'll be, Annie. I'm assuming the police will be the ones to notify George's family, and since Sally Wright is your friend, you may want to go with them to provide moral support. Why don't I take Gretchen home with me instead? I can stop at your house on the way and get some food and a couple of toys, and if necessary, I can keep her overnight. She likes to visit and enjoys playing with Matilda. In fact, I've never seen a cat and dog so compatible."

Annie thanked her friend and hugged her. She explained where she kept the dog food and Gretchen's toys and noted that plastic containers and bags were stored in the same closet. She promised she'd call her later with an update.

Chapter 9

As the sound of the sirens got closer, Suzanne led Gretchen away while Annie watched as Mike Garfield's van and an ambulance converged on the scene. Her hands still shaking and face ashen, she managed, with difficulty, to compose herself. The medical examiner walked over to her and asked that she wait for the police, who were on their way. She directed him and the EMTs to the path that led to the site.

Seconds later, a patrol car careened around a corner and parked. The police chief, Carrie Ramos, opened the door and got out. Tall and lean with topaz-colored eyes and shiny, light brown hair pulled into a ponytail low on her neck, she asked Annie why she'd been at the cemetery and how she'd discovered George's body.

Annie gave a detailed account of the sequence of events, including the message she'd received from George that morning. Since she and Suzanne had already planned to walk that afternoon, she'd invited her to come along.

Carrie responded, "That's why I saw her with Gretchen a few minutes ago."

"Yes, after we discovered George's body, Gretchen became skittish and hard to control. Suzanne's taking her home with her."

"It's fortunate that you decided to meet him here this afternoon, Annie. If you hadn't, his wife most likely would have called us this evening when he didn't return home, but even if we started looking for him immediately, it might have taken a day or two to find him. By then, the wildlife and buzzards would have done so much damage to his remains that cause of death would be difficult to determine."

She continued, "You said he found something he wanted to show you. Any idea what it was?"

"No. He sounded excited but wasn't specific; for some reason I think it may have been a relic or artifact. Cell phone reception around here isn't great, and his message was a bit garbled. Unfortunately, I deleted it after listening to it.

"For all I know, he might have just wanted to show me the damaged headstones or the terrible condition of the cemetery. He mentioned something about helping to clean it up."

Annie paused, then asked, "Wouldn't Brad typically be the one to respond to a call like this, especially since there's no indication of foul play?"

Carrie explained, "Yes, but Brad's not on duty today, he's taking courses at Finger Lakes Community College for his detective certification. I couldn't send Mia Chen, our rookie. She's spending the afternoon completing paperwork and doesn't have the experience to handle something like this."

She continued, "After his body is transported to the morgue, I'll need to notify George's wife. I'm certified as a grief counselor, but I've never had to do this before. I'm a bit apprehensive about it."

Until a few months ago, Carrie had been the deputy police chief. She'd been promoted after the former chief, Ben Fisher, moved with his wife to Arizona to be closer to her widowed mother and their two children, a daughter who was a student at the University of Arizona in Tucson, and a son who worked as an architect in Phoenix. Ben now served as chief of police in Casa Grande, a small town located midway between the two cities.

"Carrie, Sally is a dear friend. I'd like to come with you and stay until her daughter and family arrive. They live in Brighton. It's almost rush hour, and it will take them close to an hour to get here."

"Thanks. I'll take you up on your offer; it'll be nice to have the support." She took a deep breath. "I'm going to walk back to the site to speak with Mike to see if he's been able to determine the time and cause of death. Would you like to join me, or will it be too upsetting for you?"

Annie, despite feeling anxious, agreed to accompany the police chief. They reached the cemetery just as the medical examiner was completing his examination. He certified that George had died between late morning and early afternoon and announced that while it seemed as though he may have had a heart attack, the rash and vomit concerned him. He collected a sample of it and advised Carrie that she might want to consider securing the site as a crime scene, a precaution pending different results from the autopsy he planned to conduct.

The police chief ran back to the road to retrieve a plastic evidence bag and a roll of yellow crime tape from her vehicle. After donning gloves and booties, she gathered up George's personal effects, including his cellphone, wallet and keys, and handed the to-go cup to Mike. The rake, shovel and spade would remain there to be inspected later for blood and hair samples and fingerprints.

The EMTs placed George's body on a gurney; the ambulance would transport it to the morgue. Carrie taped off the area; she and Annie walked back to the road and she called the sheriff's office, requesting they send a couple of forensic technologists to the site as soon as possible. It would be dark in just a few hours. Then she called Mia.

"Mia, this is Chief Ramos." She explained the situation and asked the rookie to meet her by the path that led to the cemetery. Several minutes later when Mia arrived, Carrie handed her the bag with George's personal belongings and instructed her to wait for the technologists and assist them with their investigation.

Chapter 10

Annie and Carrie pulled into the Wright's pea gravel driveway and parked in front of a detached garage that had been constructed to replicate the style of the 1850s home that sat at the top of a hill overlooking the bay. The yard was surrounded by fragrant bayberry bushes, reminiscent of Colonial Williamsburg. A brick walk ended with several steps leading to a broad, columned porch where two white wooden rocking chairs perched on either side of the front door.

Carrie pulled the brass pineapple knocker and rapped it against the door three times. Within seconds, Sally Wright opened it. She smiled when she saw Annie.

"Oh, my, Annie, what a pleasant surprise," she exclaimed. "Please come in. I was just about to call George to see where he is. I spent the day with Lily in Skaneateles. She dropped me off about an hour ago. His truck's not here, and I expected him to be home by now." Then she noticed Carrie, who was in uniform, and with a puzzled look on her face, asked, "Aren't you the police chief, the one who replaced Ben Fisher?"

"Yes, ma'am, I am. Annie and I would like to speak with you."

Sally ushered them in and put her hand to her chest. With abject fear in her eyes, she asked, "It's Lily, isn't it? Was she in an accident on her way home? Oh my, is she dead?"

Annie quietly answered, "Sally, it's not Lily, as far as we know, she's fine. Let's go sit down." She guided her friend into the living room and sat with her on the sofa, taking her hand, while Carrie perched on a large armchair across from the pair.

Despite her anxiety, Annie said, "Sally, I'm so sorry to tell you that Suzanne Gordon and I found George's body about an hour ago in the cemetery where the casualties of the War of 1812 are buried." She explained the circumstances.

Sally cried. "I can't believe this is happening. Where is he now?"

"His body has been transported to the medical examiner's office," Carrie responded. "It appears he may have died of a heart attack, but the cause of death won't conclusively be determined until Mike conducts the autopsy. Did he have any health issues?"

Sally shook her head. "Nothing major. He took a low dose of a beta blocker for a mild case of atrial fibrillation; other than that, George was healthy. He had a physical not too long ago. His blood pressure and cholesterol levels were normal, and he passed his stress test with flying colors. He couldn't have died of a heart attack; something else must have happened to him." She placed her hands over her face and sobbed.

Annie stroked her friend's hand. "I understand how shocking this must be for you. May I call Lily? I'll stay until she gets here."

Sally nodded and continued crying while Annie called Sally's daughter. As she was speaking to her, Carrie's cell phone rang. It was the medical examiner.

Carrie stood up and walked into the foyer.

"Hi, Mike. Annie and I are with Sally Wright. Naturally, she's quite upset. What's up?"

Mike responded, "I've examined George and can give you a preliminary report, but until I have results from the autopsy and tox screen, I won't know for certain the cause of death. A person can experience nausea and get sick to their stomach with a heart attack, but that rash on his body still bothers me; that's not typical. He doesn't appear to have been mugged, as you know his personal effects were with him along with a wrapped piece of pastry in his jeans pocket and a to-go cup with some liquid in it."

"Could he have died of food poisoning? What about a food allergy?"

"It's possible. I'd appreciate your checking with Mrs. Wright, although I'm still going to have the contents of the to-go cup and pastry analyzed regardless of what she tells you."

"Okay."

"Also, please ask her whether he had any serious medical conditions."

"I already did. She said he had a mild form of AFib that was being controlled by a low dose of a beta blocker, but he had no other health issues. Could the AFib be the cause of death?"

"If it was a mild case, then probably not, but again, I won't know for certain until I conduct the autopsy."

"Anything else you need?"

"Yes, I'll need the name of the funeral home she'd like me to contact once I'm finished here."

Carrie walked back into the living room. "Mrs. Wright, Mike found a piece of pastry in George's pocket and some sort of beverage in a to-go cup and will have them analyzed, but it would be helpful to know if he had any food allergies or may have eaten something this morning that could have made him ill."

"George had no food allergies, and I can't imagine he died of food poisoning. He baked Morning Glory muffins last night for our breakfast this morning. I ate one, he ate two, and I felt fine all day. I wasn't paying attention, but I would assume he didn't finish his second one and wrapped it up. He may have wanted it as a snack for later this morning. That's probably what

Dr. Garfield found," she responded. "I'll check to see if he took it along with him."

Sally walked into the kitchen and returned to the living room within seconds. "The muffin is still here. He must have grabbed something at Bistro Louise or one of the other local restaurants that serves breakfast. I expect that's where he also purchased the beverage. He drank a cup or two of coffee in the morning, then in warmer months switched to iced tea. That's probably what's in the cup."

Carrie asked for the name of the funeral home, excused herself and walked outside to call Mike. She gave him the information he'd requested, then came back inside the house.

Annie reported that she'd spoken with Lily, who distraught upon hearing the news about her father, promised to be back in Lighthouse Cove with her family within the hour.

Offering condolences again, Carrie excused herself and drove back to the police station, and Annie went into the kitchen to get her friend a glass of water. After taking a few sips, Sally commented that she'd have to notify George's parents about his death. She feared telling them; she'd wait until Lily and her family arrived.

Lily, Eric and their two children rushed into the house an hour later. The family hugged and cried. The younger woman was inconsolable, blaming herself for not inviting her father to join her and her mother that day. She believed that if he'd had a heart attack, a quick call to 911 might have saved him. Despite her own sorrow, Sally reassured her daughter that George's death was not her fault and calling 911 might not have changed the outcome.

Hugging Sally, Annie promised to stay in touch. She quietly let herself out to walk the short distance to her home and once inside, sat down on the sofa in the living room and for several minutes sobbed over the loss of her and Ed's dear friend. Like Lily, she felt guilty and believed, despite what Sally had said, that if she'd been willing to get her sandals dirty at lunchtime, George might still be alive.

Chapter 11

After drying her eyes, Annie called Suzanne with an update.

"This has been a terrible day, Annie. Would you like to cancel our dinner for tonight? Instead, you're welcome to come to my house, I can easily fix something." She paused. "I'll also understand if you don't feel like eating and want to be alone."

"Let's stay with our original plan, Suzanne. I bought ingredients for a simple meal, and cooking will take my mind off what happened to George. Plus, I want to see Gretchen, being with her is very comforting. How's she doing?"

"She's been great. She and Matilda chased each other around for a while. She chewed on her bone and after I fed her, I let her out in the backyard for a few minutes. Right now, she's sound asleep and snoring loudly on the love seat in the living room."

Annie smiled, visualizing her 20-pound animal with a snore that sometimes sounded like that of a 200-pound man. "It's almost 6:00. I'll uncork the bottle of Pinot Grigio that's been chilling in the refrigerator, take the cheese out to warm to room temperature and start prepping for dinner. Come over as soon as you're ready. It *has* been an awful day, and I'll enjoy spending time with you."

At 8:00, just as the friends had finished eating, Annie heard the back door open.

"Hi, Annie, I'm home," Ed called out to his wife of forty-three years.

Gretchen, who'd been sleeping on Annie's foot under the kitchen table, awoke upon hearing Ed's voice, and, tail wagging, ran out of the room to greet him.

The tall, lanky, white-haired man knelt to pet her then walked into the kitchen, kissed Annie, and seeing Suzanne, reached out to give her a hug. "What a nice surprise." He smiled, his clear blue eyes shining.

Rather than plying Ed with a multitude of questions as she normally did after he returned from a consulting engagement, Annie asked quietly, "Have you eaten yet, Ed?"

"I stopped for coffee and a cookie at a travel station in Fulton; other than that I've had nothing since lunch. Is there enough for me?"

"There is, and it's warming in the oven."

"You seem unusually quiet tonight, Annie. Are you okay?"

"Why don't you get yourself a scotch? We need to talk."

Twenty minutes later, after Suzanne had helped Annie clean up the kitchen and then gone home, the pair sat on matching cocoa-colored oversized leather chairs in the living room, Ed nursing a second scotch and Annie sipping a cup of chamomile tea. The evening, as evenings do along the lake in the spring, had turned chilly. Ed lit a small fire in the fireplace.

Gretchen, sensing something was awry, and worrying that perhaps she had caused it, jumped up on Annie's lap, gave her mistress a beseeching look and licked her face. After receiving reassurance that she'd done nothing wrong, she lay down and curled up in a small ball and quickly fell asleep, this time snoring softly, a sound surprisingly calming to the couple who sat quietly without speaking.

Chapter 12

Carrie Ramos' phone rang at 11:00 the next morning. Recognizing the caller ID, she answered, "Hi, Mike. What's up?"

"Hi, Carrie, I've completed the autopsy, and have results from the tox screen."

"Was there any evidence of food poisoning or an allergic reaction?"

"No. George died of a heart attack, from a lethal combination of a beta blocker and digitalis. It's unusual for a doctor to prescribe both for a mild case of atrial fibrillation but not without precedent. I believe he may have accidentally overdosed on the digitalis, which would explain the rash and the vomit. The cup contained that drug along with iced tea."

"Mike, George wasn't taking digitalis. Remember I told you that Sally said George's AFib was being treated with a low dose of a beta blocker?" Carrie responded.

Mike paused for a second. "That's right, you did. I forgot. She didn't mention digitalis?"

"Nope."

"How curious. Carrie, could you call Mrs. Wright? Before I issue my final report, I need more information," he explained.

"I'll call her right now," Carrie promised.

She dialed the Wright's phone number. "Mrs. Wright, it's Carrie Ramos. How are you holding up?"

"None of us slept a wink last night, and my emotions are all over the place. One moment I'm crying and the next, I'm in denial and hoping this is all a terrible dream. We told George's parents last night; they're devastated. Lily and her family are with them now."

"I'm terribly sorry to disturb you. This must be so difficult, but I have some additional questions. Mike Garfield completed the autopsy and has the results from the tox screen, but he needs a little more information before he issues his formal report."

"Yes, of course."

"You mentioned George was taking a beta blocker to control his atrial fibrillation. Is it possible that his doctor also prescribed digitalis?"

"No, not that I'm aware of. What's this about?"

Carrie explained and asked Sally to check her husband's prescriptions. Putting her on hold, the woman walked upstairs, and after a few minutes returned and reported there were no bottles of digitalis, only the beta blocker.

"Where do you purchase your prescriptions?" Carrie asked.

"Our prescriptions are filled at Lattimore's; they give us a fair price and we like supporting local businesses. Does Dr. Garfield believe a mixture of the two drugs are what killed George?"

"Possibly."

"As I said, I couldn't find a prescription for digitalis."

"Mike plans to email death certificates to both George's doctor and the pharmacy this morning; after that I plan to interview them. I have Lattimore's phone number. Can you give me the doctor's contact information? Despite your assurances that George was only taking a beta blocker, I'm still going to call and ask whether they have a record of someone prescribing the second drug."

Thirty minutes later, after speaking with the doctor and the pharmacist, Carrie called Mike with a summary of her conversations.

Mike listened quietly until Carrie finished. His voice somber, he replied, "Carrie, given the information you've just provided, I'm going to go on record that George was murdered. I believe someone he met the day he died knew about his condition and that combining the two drugs would be lethal."

Carrie sighed. "I was afraid of that. I'll call Sally and let her know. Thanks, Mike."

Sally cried for several seconds, then collected herself. "I'm not surprised. I knew he wasn't ill, although I can't imagine why anyone would have wanted to kill him." She took a breath. "He's to be cremated. Our family would like to do that as soon as Dr. Garfield releases his body."

"George's body can go to the funeral home any time, Mrs. Wright. I'll ask Mike to call and make arrangements for them to pick him up."

Chapter 13

Carrie wasn't happy; truth be told, she was somewhat unnerved. She was short-handed with Brad taking classes and Mia, her rookie, not experienced enough to investigate a murder on her own. The criminal technologists had called and reported that no prints other than George's were in his truck or on any of his tools or personal effects, and there were no blood or hair samples that couldn't be identified. The mud had made it impossible to make decent impressions of footprints.

While one of the techs drove George's truck back to the Wright's house, others stayed at the site. They were able to identify tire tracks belonging to the emergency and police vehicles, and Annie DeCleryk's and Jason Shipley's cars, but not another set, from what appeared to be a sports car.

Other than Carrie's husband, Matt, no one else knew she was pregnant with their second child. She was experiencing morning sickness and feeling overwhelmed. With money in the budget for miscellaneous expenses, she decided to call Ed DeCleryk, hoping he would be willing to investigate George's murder.

Carrie dialed his number. The phone rang, and he picked up immediately.

"Ed, it's Carrie."

"Hi, Carrie. What can I do for you?"

"Can you meet me at Bistro Louise later this morning?" The bistro had become the preferred meeting place for Ed, Carrie, and the former police chief, Ben Fisher, during the months Ed had investigated Emily Bradford's murder.

"Mike Garfield completed George's autopsy. I'd like to speak with you about it."

Ed explained that he'd just applied the final coat of varnish to the vintage boat he'd been restoring and was wearing an old tee shirt, paint-spattered shorts and ratty sneakers. He needed to wipe the paint off his hands, shower and put on clean clothes. "I'll meet you in an hour. I can't imagine you'd want me to show up looking like this."

Chapter 14

Ed and Carrie arrived simultaneously at the bistro. The morning breakfast crowd had thinned, and it was too early for lunch. They secured a table next to a window that overlooked the lake. Gentle waves lapped onto the shore, a few sailboats bobbed about the water, and a tugboat chugged lazily past the pier where the towered lighthouse stood. They watched as a few young mothers and their small children scooped up colorful rocks and small, pearly freshwater oyster shells from the beach and deposited them into colorful plastic buckets.

Terri, the pretty red-haired server who was dressed in black leggings, white sneakers and a long white tee shirt with the bistro's logo, approached their table.

"Hi, guys, seeing you together must mean something bad is going on. Has another heinous crime been committed?" she asked with wide smile.

"If there were, we wouldn't be able to talk about it with you, Terri," Carrie admonished, then changed the subject. "What are the pastry specials today?"

Ignoring Carrie's question, Terry responded, "I heard about George Wright's death." She paused for a second. "Oh, my, was George murdered? This village can't take another murder. Emily's was tough enough, especially given how...."

Carrie interrupted her. "Terri. Stop. I really, really can't say anything about this right now."

Terri shrugged, took a deep breath, and turning chilly announced that the owner, Louise, had baked some fresh baguettes and crusty rolls earlier that morning, whole grain and sourdough, and had just removed lemon blueberry scones from the oven. She had also made some fresh lemon curd.

Carrie licked her lips. She'd eaten breakfast before coming to work that morning but, as with the early months of her last pregnancy, was always starving. She laughed, "While I'd love one of each, my waistline wouldn't. I'll have a crusty whole grain roll with no butter and raspberry preserves, if you have any."

"And to drink?" Terri asked politely, displeased she'd been rebuffed.

"I'll have a decaf latte with skim milk, no sugar or flavor shots," she replied.

Terri looked at Ed, arching an eyebrow. "And you?"

Bemused, Ed responded, "I'm not watching my waistline. I'll have two scones with the lemon curd, and a cup of high-test cappuccino with whole milk." He grinned at Carrie, "and a hazelnut shot." In response, Carrie rolled her eyes.

Without saying another word, Terri walked away, her bearing haughty.

Ed laughed. "She's certainly in a snit."

"She'll get over it. She was pretty upset after Emily's murder. Remember, she had a huge crush on...." Before completing her sentence, her cell phone, which she'd placed on the table in front of her, chimed with an incoming text message. She read it, and thumbs flying on the keyboard, responded. Then she looked at Ed.

"That was Matt. I've been unusually tired lately, and to save me a trip to the market he offered to stop on his way home from work. I texted him with a short list." Carrie's husband, Matt Ramos, was an emergency room doctor at the local hospital and had recently shifted from working nights to days, enabling him to be at home during the evening to help with their 18-month-old daughter, Natalya, and on the rare occasions that Carrie was called out to visit a crime scene.

Ed, with a twinkle in his eye, remarked, "Carrie, why are you so tired, and why are you being so careful about what you ordered? You usually eat like a stevedore and never gain a pound. Anything you want to tell me?"

Carrie sighed, then laughed. "Nothing much gets past you, Ed. I'm pregnant."

"That's wonderful, Carrie. Congratulations. Besides being tired, are you feeling okay? May I share the happy news with Annie?"

"I'm doing fine, although half the time I'm nauseous and half the time I'm ravenous. I didn't experience these extremes when I was pregnant with Natalya, and I'm trying to be careful about what I eat so I don't gain too much weight. Go ahead and tell Annie, but please ask her to keep this confidential. We're not going to notify our parents until I complete the first trimester."

"Annie keeps confidences, Carrie. Remember, I didn't even know about Emily Bradford's $500,000 endowment to the museum until after her death. I couldn't believe Annie would withhold that information from me, but she did because Emily asked her to. Your secret's safe with us."

Carrie smiled and thanked Ed, and the pair chatted amiably for a couple of minutes while waiting for Terri to reappear with their order. After they were served, Carrie announced, "George died of heart failure, Ed, most likely after ingesting a fatal combination of a beta blocker and digitalis. Mike believes he was murdered."

She continued, "I'm shorthanded right now with Brad taking courses at FLCC for his detective certification, and I'm training a new rookie. The village trustees have decided to hold off funding for a deputy police chief; instead we've signed an agreement with the county sheriff's office for backup coverage. To pacify me, they increased my budget so I can hire consultants if needed. They probably thought I'd never spend it. But here we are again with another murder. Would you be willing to investigate it? Hopefully it won't take as long to solve as Emily's did."

Ed responded, "George was a close friend."

"I know."

"Sally's distraught, and both Annie and I are immeasurably sad about his death. I'd definitely like to be involved in finding his killer."

"Can you start today?"

"I'll start as soon as we finish our meeting."

Carrie continued, "Sally and Lily have alibis, and Lily said her husband, Eric, was working from home most of the day; for now, we can probably rule out family members as suspects. I spoke with George's doctor, Maria Cisneros, who confirmed he was taking a beta blocker for atrial fibrillation, not digitalis. She acknowledged that as mild as his condition was, combining that with the beta blocker would have been fatal."

"Carrie, despite what George's doctor told you, I'm still going to schedule an appointment with her. She may not have prescribed digitalis, but it's possible someone else at the practice, someone who wanted him dead, may have given him a sample."

Chapter 15

Ed walked to his car and called Annie to tell her Carrie had hired him to investigate George's murder. When she didn't pick up, he remembered that she had a meeting with the executive director of the historical society in Pultneyville to discuss working on some joint projects. He left a message.

He then called George's doctor's office, hoping to speak with her that afternoon. Her receptionist explained that Dr. Cisneros was seeing patients until six o'clock and after, planned to attend a function at her children's school. He made an appointment for 9:00 the next morning.

The windows in Ed's study had views of the water, and now back at home as he sat at his desk making notes for the interview, he spied a bald eagle, one of several he'd observed nesting along the lakefront. He assumed she was searching for food for her recently hatched eaglets; he'd viewed them with his binoculars on a hike along the bluff one morning. He'd read somewhere that Native Americans viewed the eagle as a symbol of strength and courage; he equated those same traits to George.

He called Annie again, anxious to speak with her. This time she picked up on the second ring.

"Hi, honey. Just checking in."

"Hi. I got your voice message. Sorry I didn't return your call; I've been pretty tied up all day. Are you sure you want to be the one to investigate George's murder? That's going to be emotionally very difficult for you."

"I thought about it. I'll be fine. I want to have the satisfaction of finding his killer and making sure he's put away for life. How's your day going?"

"Okay, I guess, given the circumstances, though I had a good meeting with Tom Laughlin. We're going to work together on a Christmas tour of historical homes, and I'm excited about that. His intern is gathering a list of the properties that would qualify, and I expect within the next couple of weeks we'll be ready to draft a letter asking for participation. We believe if we move quickly, we can make it happen this year."

"That'll be something to look forward to over the holidays. How's Jason coming along with his project?"

"He's almost finished writing the brochure on the War of 1812. He met with Amanda the day of George's murder and took lots of notes and is making good progress. I've scheduled a history talk about that war for the fall and am planning to invite her to speak about her book. I can distribute the brochures at the same time."

"When will you be home?"

"Missing me?"

"Yes, a little. I'm sad about George. His death has made me acutely aware of how fragile life is. I don't want to be maudlin, but I think I'd feel comforted today with your presence."

"I have plans to take lunch to Sally and Lily, who's staying with her mother for a few days, Ed. George was cremated this morning, and they're heartbroken. They've asked me to help plan the memorial service for the end of the week. I can come home after that instead of going back to work. Will you be okay until then?"

"Of course."

"What's happening with the investigation?"

"I have an appointment with George's doctor tomorrow morning and called my Navy buddies who gave me an update on their lunch together. They said that George never showed up, and, of course, all of them have alibis. I just started putting notes together with a list of other possible suspects. That should keep me busy for a while."

Ed was at his desk, Gretchen sleeping on the floor beside him, when Annie walked into his study at 2:00. She bent down to pat the dog and the beagle opened her eyes and wagged her tail. She then kissed Ed, who stood up and hugged her.

"How are you?" she asked.

"Very sad, but I've made some progress. I've gone about as far as I can go for now. What's happening at Sally's?"

"We planned the service for Friday at the Peace Church. It will be a small group; family, close friends, some co-workers, and Carrie, if she's able to attend. Sally doesn't want much fanfare, although she's agreed to an abbreviated military service. The funeral home is obtaining an American flag, and she's requested that you present it to her, Ed."

Ed, his throat thick with emotion, nodded, unable to speak. Tears glistened in his eyes. He took a couple of deep breaths.

"Did Sally say how George's parents are doing?"

"Yes. They're in bad shape. As you're aware, they're both in failing health and have almost round-the-clock care at their cottage. George and Sally wanted them to be able to stay in their home, although Sally thinks that the blow of dealing with George's death may hasten their decline and force a move into a continuing care facility."

"I'm fond of them and while not surprised, sorry to hear that." Ed paused. "Since this has been such a busy and emotional day for us, would you like to go out to dinner?"

Annie replied, "Actually, I think I'd like to stay in. I don't think I can handle the noise in a restaurant tonight, and we don't need to deal with nosy patrons who'll be curious about George's death. Instead, let's set up the table on the back porch, light a fire in the fire pit, and I'll cook something simple."

"I like that idea."

"Any requests?"

"How about a steak and that French potato salad you make and green beans with tarragon. We have a bottle of Parisi Cabernet Franc in the wine cellar. I'll bring it up."

"That's perfect, Ed. I'll run over to the market to get ingredients and be back soon."

Chapter 16

At 9:00 the next morning after a short drive to Wolcott, a small town that sat at the edge of Port Bay east of Lighthouse Cove, Ed entered the building where the medical practice was located. Irwin Shaw, the practice manager, had been waiting at the receptionist's desk and introduced himself. The two men shook hands then the elegantly dressed ebony-skinned man escorted Ed to Dr. Cisneros' office.

A framed photo of the doctor with her arm around two smiling teenagers sat on the dark maple desk that faced the door, and framed degrees hung on the wall behind it. To the right of the desk, a round, wooden conference table and four ladder-backed chairs sat in front of a bookshelf filled with medical texts.

The doctor, a tall, lean, middle-aged woman with graying chin-length hair and warm brown eyes, was sitting at the table. She stood up, shook Ed's hand and motioned for the two men to join her.

"I'm terribly sorry about George Wright."

"We were close friends," Ed replied. "I've known him since childhood."

"Then I'm doubly sorry. How can I help you?"

Ed explained the circumstances of George's death to the pair. "You're aware that a combination of two drugs killed George?"

The doctor answered, "I am. Your police chief called, but the only drug I prescribed was the beta blocker, and I lowered the dosage after his last checkup, which was two weeks ago."

"Did he see anyone else in the practice who might have given a sample to him?"

"Doug Logan, our physician's assistant, and I are the only ones who examined him. Doug's been on family medical leave for three weeks; in his absence we've hired another PA, Mary Williams, from a medical employment agency. She's popular with our patients and our practice is growing; we're considering hiring her full-time. I don't believe Mary had any interaction with George in Doug's absence, but would you like to speak with her?"

"Yes, but I'd prefer to do it privately."

Irwin responded, "Once we're finished here, I'll go see if she's with a patient; if she's free you can use our conference room."

Despite what the doctor had reported, Ed was curious if there might be a connection between the PA and his friend. He asked, "Has George been in the office since his last checkup?"

"He has," Dr. Cisneros replied, after opening her computer and scrolling down several pages. "A couple days before he died. He was planning to take an advanced cardio exercise program that begins June 1 at the recreation center in Lighthouse Cove. His instructor required me to sign off on it, which I did. He probably wasn't here more than fifteen minutes."

"Was Mary Williams in the office that day?"

Irwin, who'd been carrying an iPad, scrolled to his calendar. "She was."

"What about the day George was killed? Was she in that day?"

"Yes, but not until 12:30. We had evening hours and she worked until 8:30 that night."

"Giving her time and opportunity to kill George that morning," Ed thought," *but how did they know each other and what would her motive have been?"*

Dr. Cisneros asked, "You aren't really considering Mary as a suspect, are you?"

"I won't know until I interview her." He looked at Irwin. "Could you please see if she's available to speak with me?"

Irwin left the room and within a couple minutes returned, looking concerned.

"She didn't sign in this morning. I assumed she came in early to see a patient and forgot, that happens sometimes. I knocked on her door; when she didn't answer, I opened it. She wasn't there, and no one's seen her today. I've asked our receptionist to contact the temp agency. Perhaps she called in sick and for some reason they didn't notify us."

A few minutes later, the doctor's phone buzzed, and she answered it. "Yes, thanks. That's concerning. Did they try her at home?" After a few seconds, she hung up the phone and looked at Ed and Irwin.

"She never called in. The temp agency called her home and cell phones while our receptionist waited on another line, and no one answered."

"Do you keep drugs here?" Ed inquired.

"Yes," the doctor answered, "a limited supply, mainly samples from pharmaceutical companies of non-narcotics like antibiotics and decongestants. They're stored in a walk-in supply closet."

"Who has access to them?"

"Doug, Mary, and I are the only ones who're authorized to remove the drugs from the closet; we all have keys. Irwin also has a key, but since he doesn't see patients, that's just to check inventory. Our office staff and nurses have no access to that closet."

Ed asked, "When someone takes a drug, do they sign off on it? How often do you check the inventory?"

Irwin answered, "Yes, there's a sheet of paper tacked to a clipboard that's hanging on the wall inside the closet. When someone removes a drug, they sign their name, date, the drug and quantity and the patient's name and reason for administering it. I check inventory once a week."

"Is digitalis one of the drugs?"

Irwin acknowledged that they kept a small supply of digitalis and blood thinners in addition to the other drugs; then, after Ed requested, excused himself to check the inventory. While he was gone, Ed and the doctor made small talk.

After a few minutes, Irwin walked back into the office. "Mary is the only one who's taken drugs from that closet over the past couple weeks. A few days ago, she took a bottle each of digitalis and a blood thinner for one of our other patients, not George."

"Then it appears her absence today is not related to my case and there's no point in my speaking with her. Since no one else here had any opportunity to give George the digitalis, I'll be on my way." Ed stood up to leave. "I'm sorry to have taken so much of your time."

The practice manager answered, "Please don't go just yet. I haven't quite finished. For some reason, I was suspicious, I'm not sure why, so I read the chart of the patient she supposedly gave the drugs to and discovered that Doug has never prescribed either of them for him. The man doesn't have a heart problem.

"Then I checked the computer at the receptionist's desk to make sure he had an appointment that day. He did, but it was for a sore throat and low-grade fever. Mary's follow-up notes in his chart indicated she diagnosed it as a virus. She recommended gargling with saltwater and taking an over-the-counter medicine for the fever."

He continued, "As much as I hate to believe it, it appears Mary stole the drugs; perhaps that's why she didn't report to work today. She came highly recommended, but we expect the temp agency to do the background checks for us. We don't know all that much about her."

"You're positive the signature is hers?"

"I am. She retrieved an antibiotic from the closet last week. It was for a patient she'd diagnosed with bronchitis. I checked the woman's chart, and it verified she had an appointment with Mary that day for a respiratory problem. I compared the two signatures. They match."

Ed replied, "It's puzzling; still; let's not jump to conclusions. The evidence pointing to her being involved in killing George is circumstantial. The tox screen showed digitalis in his system, but no blood thinner, and I don't want to rush to judgement. There may be a very reasonable explanation for why she took the drugs that's unrelated to her absence today."

He continued, "Maybe she's ill or had a family emergency and couldn't get to a phone. I'd still like to interview her, but mostly to rule her out as a suspect. Could you please give me Mary's contact information? In the meantime, I'd appreciate your calling me if you hear from her." He retrieved two business cards from his jacket pocket and handed them to the pair.

The doctor and practice manager nodded. Irwin left the office and reappeared a few minutes later with Mary Williams' address and phone numbers. Ed thanked them for their cooperation and exited the building. Once back inside his car, he called Carrie.

Chapter 17

"Hi, Carrie; it's Ed. "

"Hi, Ed. Are you still at the doctor's office?"

"Just finished." He summarized the meeting and said that although he'd follow up with an interview, he believed there was another reason that Mary Williams took the drugs. He gave Carrie her address and asked that she run a background check, just in case there was something he was missing.

"I can probably get something superficial in a matter of hours, Ed. A more in-depth report could take several weeks."

"Do the quick one first. I'd like to interview her as soon as possible."

"Okay. I'll call as soon as I have any information."

Ed took scenic Orchard Lane back to Lighthouse Cove instead of the highway. The road meandered through wetlands and orchards with pretty wood-framed farmhouses dotting the landscape, many painted in pastels that matched the blooming trees and spring flowers. As he neared Lighthouse Cove, he crossed a one-lane bridge where he observed fishermen unloading baskets of fish at the sprawling cedar-sided market facing the bay.

He stopped at the small, roadside stand that sat on a small plot of land at the corner of Orchard and Brick Church Road and purchased a wedge of sharp cheese from the large round that sat on the countertop and an apple pie, presumably made with apples that had sat in cold storage over the winter.

As he approached his house, he could see Annie's car in the driveway, and he felt warmth spreading across his chest, pleased his beloved wife was home. George's death had shaken him more than he realized, and he felt a swell of gratitude for the days he shared with her and their family, understanding how fleeting life can be.

The back door was unlocked, and as Ed entered the house, Gretchen, who'd been sleeping soundly on her bed in the kitchen, awoke and began growling. Then she realized the 'intruder' was Ed and stretching, she wagged her tail, sidled up to him for a kiss and flopped on her back for a belly rub. Annie entered the room just as Ed was placing the pie and cheese in the refrigerator.

"Oh, you startled me, Ed. I didn't expect you home quite this early." Ed kissed the top of her head.

"I just got back from the interview at George's doctor's office and am waiting for a call from Carrie. It's a long shot, but one of their medical staff may be a person of interest. Before I go any farther, I asked her to run a background check."

"I'm glad you're home. I hope this person is the murderer, so you can solve the case before we go to England next month."

The previous spring, months after Emily Bradford's murderer had been arrested, Ed had taken his metal detector to the beach and uncovered a rusted box with pieces of jewelry and other trinkets inside. Upon verification from Cornell University and experts from England, it had been determined that the box contained valuables belonging to the British monarchy that had been stolen by a cabin boy, named Thomas Battleforth, who had escaped during a shipwreck on the lake in the 1700s.

Ed had contacted the U. S. State Department, and working with its counterpart in England, they sent the treasure back to where it belonged. In appreciation, he and Annie had been invited by the British government, all expenses paid, to view the restored, jewel-encrusted, pieces that were now on display at the Victoria and Albert museum in London.

Annie's British friend, Donna Jones, the former director of the Lighthouse Cove Museum and Historical Society, had moved back to England with her husband, Ross, a retired U. S. Air Force officer, and now served as the museum's curator of special exhibits.

Annie and Ed had decided to extend their stay at their own expense to take some side trips and to see a couple plays in the theatre district, which was within walking distance of their hotel in Covent Gardens. The last weekend there they planned a trip to Paris with Donna and her husband.

Ed responded, "Me, too. Did you close shop early?"

"No. A couple of our docents are giving a tour, and I managed to slip home to grab something to eat and check on Gretchen. I wasn't sure how long you'd be, and I hadn't arranged for Sandy to come and let her out. I need to get back."

"Sandy's a fabulous pet sitter and like a second mom to Gretchen, but I expect our puppy was overjoyed to see you." Annie smiled in response. Ed continued, "Anything exciting going on?"

"Yes!" She beamed. "It's such a clear day that I climbed up to the widow's walk with my binoculars. I spotted a huge cruise ship along the horizon, and a couple of freighters. I guess that means spring is finally here to stay."

"Despite the specter of George's death hanging over us, I'm glad the weather has turned." Ed changed the subject. "Have you started to prepare dinner yet?"

"No. Let's go out, but I'd prefer not to stay in the village. If we eat here, curious friends and neighbors will bombard us with questions about the murder."

"Where would you like to go?"

"How about Rum Runners? The drive along the lake will be beautiful, and I love the atmosphere and food."

"I'll make a reservation for 6:30."

"I'm heading back to work but should be home by 5:00. I'll need to clean up and change my clothes, but we should still have plenty of time."

"I'll walk and feed Gretchen. See you soon."

As Annie walked out the door she turned, smiled and blew Ed a kiss.

Chapter 18

The phone rang just as Ed was finishing lunch; it was Carrie.

"Hi, Ed. I have results from the background check."

"What did you find?" he asked.

"Mary's clean; has no criminal record. She's in her early 60s, single, never married, no kids, and lives on Pear Road, a few miles south of Lighthouse Cove."

"Anything else?"

"Yes, something that might be pertinent to your investigation."

"What's that?"

"She served in the military." Carrie paused. "In the Navy, right around the time you and George were in the service, and she was stationed at Norfolk and San Diego early in her career at the same time as George. I called Sally, and she verified the dates. Mary retired after 20 years and enrolled at R.I.T. to get her physician's assistant degree.

"Any indication George was her commanding officer?"

"No. I'd have to dig deeper to get that information." She paused. "How old was George when he married Sally?"

"He was in his early 30s. Sally's several years younger. Why are you asking?"

Carrie sighed. "I know this might be a bit of a stretch, but after I read the report I started wondering if it could have been possible that George and Mary met while they were both serving in the Navy and had some sort of romantic involvement. I called Sally and asked if she remembered the names of any of the women he'd dated before they got together. She responded that they had decided not to talk about previous relationships, what was past was past, but she was aware that George had been in a relationship that had ended at about the time she'd met him."

"Where are you headed with this, Carrie?"

"If he and Mary did have a relationship, perhaps he ended it because he realized he wasn't in love with her after he met Sally. Mary might have been terribly upset and angry at first but eventually decided to put the entire episode behind her and was able to move on.

"Then their paths cross at the doctor's office. They chat, and she learns that George has led a very privileged life, with a wife and daughter he loves and financial security in retirement. She invites him for coffee, indicating there are no hard feelings; she just wants to catch up. They agree to meet at one of our local restaurants.

"But what she tells him isn't true. She's barely making ends meet working as a temp and feels angry and resentful that their lives have taken such different turns. After he leaves the office, she reads his files and learns he's on a beta blocker and determines to get revenge. She steals the digitalis and slips it into his drink the morning they meet, knowing that combining it with the beta blocker will kill him."

"Carrie, we have no proof that the relationship George ended before starting to date Sally was with Mary, but even if your hunch is correct, there's the question of the blood thinner."

"Ed, maybe she stole the blood thinner for a completely different purpose, maybe even to cast suspicion away from herself as George's murderer. Look at the facts. They both live in the area, she works at the medical practice where he was a patient; he suffered from AFib, and she stole a bottle of digitalis just days before he died of an overdose of it. That's too much coincidence," Carrie argued.

"I suppose it's possible," Ed admitted, "but George and Sally didn't keep secrets from each other, and he would have told her if he'd agreed to meet with Mary that morning."

"Then instead of bumping into each other in the office, perhaps it happened another way," Carrie insisted.

"She could have been in the office one day when he came for a checkup, recognized him, but didn't introduce herself. All the memories of what he'd done came back to her and after checking his chart, she determined to get revenge. Remember, Mary didn't arrive at work until 12:30 the day George was killed. Maybe she was having breakfast at one of our restaurants here in the village when George came in to purchase the pastry and his tea. She goes over to him and introduces herself, he's pleased to see her after all these years, and she invites him to join her."

"Do you really think she would have been carrying digitalis around with her waiting for an opportunity to poison George? That seems quite a stretch."

Carrie relented. "As I said before, maybe she stole both drugs for another purpose but for some reason had them with her that morning and killing him was not premeditated. The longer they talked, the more resentful she became. Perhaps he went to the bathroom or was distracted by something and that's when she spiked his drink."

"I'm going to drive over to her house this morning; hopefully she'll be there and be receptive to answering my questions, and we'll get to the bottom of this."

Carrie countered, "Why not call ahead?"

"If she's there, she may not answer the phone, or if she does, she may decline to speak with me without a warrant or in the presence of an attorney. I'd like to keep this as informal as possible."

"Ed, if she killed George, she could be unstable and dangerous. I'd like to send Mia with you for backup."

"Let's not complicate this, Carrie. For some reason my instincts are telling me I won't have a problem with her."

Carrie cautioned, "If she's at home, she may be hesitant to let a man she doesn't know into her house."

"Then I'll show her my credentials and suggest she call you for verification. Trust me on this one."

"Please be careful. I'd hate for you to walk into something that could put you in harm's way. Do you still have a license to carry?"

"I do."

"Then at least let me deputize you and issue you a gun and a pair of cuffs. I'll feel better knowing you can protect yourself should you find yourself in danger, and if she confesses to killing George, you'll be able to Mirandize her and bring her in."

Ed shook his head, sighed, but weary of arguing, agreed to Carrie's request. Several minutes later, as he started walking out the door, she asked, "What if she's not at home?"

"Then I'll call you and we'll figure out what's next."

Chapter 19

Farmhouses and fruit orchards dotted the landscape along Pear Road, along with homes that had been built in the 1950s and '60s. Ed reached Mary Williams' house, a small one-story ranch with white siding and green trim, after driving about a mile down the road. A freestanding one-car garage sat at the end of a short, graveled driveway, a huge maple stood in the middle of the neatly mowed yard, and several trimmed evergreen bushes sat along the front of the house. At the end of a short walk, four steps led up to the front door. Ed pressed a doorbell and waited.

After about 30 seconds, a frail man in a wheelchair opened the door. His thinning hair was white, and his arms were dotted with age spots and bruises that appeared to be the result of taking blood thinners. He wore a clean, navy blue sport shirt, baggy gray pants and tan slippers on his feet. Ed could see a portable oxygen tank in the foyer.

"Can I help you?" he asked, with shortened breath.

"Is this the Williams' residence?" Ed asked.

"It is. I'm Albert Williams. Is there something I can do for you?"

"Maybe she took the drugs for another purpose," Carrie had said. And, Ed thought as he observed the elderly man, *Albert Williams might be that reason.* Still, Ed had to proceed with the planned purpose for his visit—to question Mary about George's death. If she stole the drugs for her father, he hoped his questioning would reveal it.

Taking his credentials out of his pocket, Ed responded, "I'm a criminal consultant with the Lighthouse Cove police department, and I'd like to speak with Mary."

A look of alarm passed briefly over the man's face. Then Ed heard a hoarse female voice whisper, "Let him in, Dad."

Williams motioned for Ed to enter. A tiny foyer opened into a small living room, spotlessly clean but careworn, that was furnished with two, faded matching green, black and beige plaid chairs with an oak side table placed between them, and across the room, a faded green sofa. A small flat screen TV sat atop an oak credenza in one corner, with an old, upright piano against a wall.

A gray-haired, pale-faced woman lay on the sofa, her nose red and eyes dripping. Despite the heat, she was wearing a quilted robe and her torso was covered with blankets. A glass filled with something fizzy sat on a coffee table in front of her.

"I don't understand why you would be checking up on me. I didn't show up for work because I have the flu. I called the agency's answering service early this morning, and they promised to call Dr. Cisneros' office to let them know I wouldn't be in.

"Our phones rang a couple hours ago, both the landline and my cell. I couldn't answer, I was helping dad get dressed. I didn't recognize the number; whoever called isn't in my contact list and they left no message."

"It appears the answering service never contacted the doctor's office to report your illness. And yes, the call came from someone at the medical practice. I'm sorry you're not feeling well, but that's not why I'm here," Ed responded. "I'm investigating the murder of George Wright."

Mary Williams looked confused. "A murder? That's terrible. Who was he?"

"He was a patient at Dr. Cisneros' office and in the Navy, stationed at Norfolk and San Diego, at the same time as you were. You're certain your paths never crossed?"

Mary looked blankly at him. "I've never met this man. Why would you think I would know anything about his murder?"

"He died of an overdose of digitalis. I'm aware you stole that drug and a blood thinner from the supply closet at the doctor's office. Can you tell me why?"

Albert Williams, who had been sitting quietly, spoke up. "Now listen here, young man. My daughter wouldn't steal drugs, and she certainly wouldn't murder anyone."

"It's okay, dad," Mary interjected, then started to cry. "He's right, I stole both drugs. But I swear to you, I didn't murder anyone. He needs to know the truth." Her father stared at her, not completely comprehending what she'd just confessed.

Mary looked at Ed and explained that her father had worked as a coal miner in northern Pennsylvania. Then, a year before he had planned to retire, her mother died, the mine went bankrupt, and he lost his pension. He'd not been feeling well, and a trip to a local medical clinic confirmed he had a multitude of serious health ailments, including a heart condition, high blood pressure and COPD.

He received a monthly Social Security check, but without his pension, his finances were strained, and his drug costs were so high that there wasn't much left to cover his other expenses. In order to make ends meet, he began drawing money from a savings account he and her mother had built up over many years.

Mary persuaded him to sell his house, roll the proceeds of the sale into his savings, and move in with her. He'd offered to help pay for some of their monthly expenses, but Mary refused. At the time, she had a secure, good-paying job and planned to support him and only use his savings for emergencies or medical costs not covered by Medicare as his health continued to deteriorate.

Their circumstances changed when she was laid off after a private health group purchased the practice where she'd been working full-time as a PA in Lyons, closed the office and merged it with another that was located more than an hour from her home.

She had filed for and received unemployment compensation, but that had ended, and she still hadn't found full-time employment, despite actively searching for months. Money was tight.

With few options, she began working for an agency that specialized in providing temporary medical personnel to local offices; none of them more than half-an-hour commute, enabling her to care for her father without the need to hire a home health care worker. She wasn't yet eligible for Medicare, and as a temp, she had no employer-paid health benefits. She was able to get insurance through COBRA, but the cost was prohibitive.

Then she experienced one financial crisis after another. Her roof needed replacing at the same time her furnace broke down, and she'd needed to purchase a new transmission for her car. Having no choice, she started accepting help from her father, using his money to cover some of his expenses, but she couldn't continue doing that much longer, the money was dwindling.

They were a private family and never confided to her father's doctor about their financial circumstances. Still, he occasionally provided Albert with drug samples, but they were typically for the less expensive ones. That helped, but their finances continued to be strained.

She decided no one would miss a bottle or two of digitalis, or the more costly blood thinner, so she took them and listed them on the inventory sheet under another patient's name. She'd never stolen drugs before and felt guilty.

"I knew as soon as I took the drugs that what I did was wrong," she sobbed, "but since I'd already signed off on them, there was no way I could return them without causing suspicion as to why I took them in the first place." She'd hoped Irwin Shaw would accept the explanation she'd given on the inventory sheet and wouldn't check further, and she vowed never to do it again.

"Mary, we've discussed this before," her father admonished. "I have money to help with my medical care. Even I know that Medicaid will pick up many of the costs should my funds be depleted. Why on earth would you steal drugs?"

"I felt desperate, Dad, and I didn't want you to have to worry. I wanted to make sure that you live comfortably as you continue to age, and I wasn't sure how long your money, or mine for that matter since I'm not working full-time, would last."

The woman was terribly distressed about what she had done and upset about her father's plight. Ed got her to agree to call Dr. Cisneros and confess to taking the drugs. He hoped that the doctor wouldn't press charges, but his job was to find George's murderer, and he didn't want to get in the middle of a petty theft case.

Chapter 20

Several minutes later, Ed left the Williams' residence and got into his car, called Carrie and made an appointment to meet with her as soon as he got back to the village.

"Coffee, tea?" Carrie asked, as he walked in the door.

"Is the coffee fresh? I'm not in the mood for tea," Ed responded.

"Probably not. I can brew some or we can skip the coffee and I can get bottled water or iced tea from the vending machine," Carrie offered.

"I'll get the water. Be back in a minute."

Once the pair had settled in chairs that sat around a small round table, Ed proceeded to describe his interview with Mary Williams. He'd ruled her out as a suspect and believed she didn't know George; whatever happened between her and Maria Cisneros was their business. Ed hoped she wouldn't end up in jail. The poor woman was distraught and needed help; not punishment.

"I've made a list, Carrie, of others I plan to interview. I have some errands to run now, so I'll start that tomorrow.

Ed's phone rang just as he was just coming out of the hardware store.

"Mr. DeCleryk, this is Maria Cisneros."

"Hello, Dr. Cisneros. What can I do for you?"

"Mary Williams called me."

"I'm glad she did," Ed responded. "She's not a suspect in the murder, and I'm assuming she confessed to stealing the drugs?"

"She did."

"I must admit to feeling sorry for the poor woman and her father."

"I do, too. I'm upset she didn't feel she could talk with me about her financial situation. She was unaware that there's a state sponsored program for income eligible seniors that would cover the cost of drugs that aren't covered by Medicare.

"I told her about it, but she said she'd been fearful of jeopardizing her employment with us if she confided in me about her circumstances. I'm not pressing charges."

"I'm glad. What happens now?"

"She's not going to lose her job. I called her former employer who gave her glowing reviews and regretted having to let her go. The temp agency reported that each medical practice she worked for before coming to us wished they'd had money to hire her full time. She's extremely competent, our patients like her, and my practice has grown. As I think I mentioned when we met, I need to hire another full-time PA."

The doctor continued, "No one is perfect, and this incident is the only blemish on her record. I've hired her, and I'll put her on our health plan. She offered to pay me back for the drugs she stole, but they were samples that cost the practice nothing.

"I've contacted our state and county offices of aging. As I thought, her father will be eligible to receive his drugs through the state, and for home health care services through the county. She'll not have to worry about him while she's at work. Of course, she'll be on probation for six months, that's just routine. I expect there will be no further incidents."

Ed, smiling at the outcome, thanked Dr. Cisneros for her follow up and told her he appreciated her compassion. The situation had been resolved exactly as he had hoped.

Chapter 21

Ed returned home. Annie was just about to get in the shower and asked Ed to let Gretchen out. Instead of relieving herself, the dog spent several minutes scouring the yard for disgusting things to eat. Ed called her back in; she ignored him. He went out with her leash, clipped it on her collar and led her back inside the house. "You are such a stubborn dog," he admonished. "It's a good thing you're so cute."

Annie appeared a few minutes later, wrapped in a large, fluffy, white terry cloth robe with a towel piled up on her head like a turban.

"Did you solve the crime?" she asked.

Ed told her about his conversation with Dr. Cisneros and her practice manager, Irwin Shaw, and his subsequent interview with Mary Williams. Annie, despite being disappointed that Ed hadn't arrested George's killer, was pleased at the outcome.

"I made a reservation for 6:30 at Rum Runner's," Ed noted. "I'm going to go upstairs and clean up and should be ready to leave about 6:00. I'm really looking forward to our evening together."

Traffic was light on Lake Road, and the couple arrived at their destination with time to spare. Annie, normally loquacious, hadn't spoken a word on the drive, seemingly lost in thought.

"Annie, you're very somber this evening. Is something wrong?"

Annie nodded. "Yes, but it has nothing to do with us, so please don't be concerned. I'll tell you about it later."

The restaurant had been a speakeasy in the 1920s and was located on a small cove, overgrown with reeds and grasses, that was the site where rum runners from Canada had smuggled spirits into New York during Prohibition.

After checking in with the hostess, the couple went to the bar. Shelves upon shelves on the wall behind it contained an impressive variety of spirits and wine; the restaurant specialized in rum drinks. Ed and Annie both ordered the signature cocktail, a delicious concoction of rum, liquors and tropical fruit juices. Annie was eerily quiet, despite Ed's attempt to draw her out.

After several minutes, the hostess escorted the pair to their table, past a small area between the bar and the dining room where comfortable lounge chairs circled a grand piano.

Windows surrounded the bright dining room on three sides. Tables of varying sizes, all with high backed rattan chairs, nestled close to one another, each with a view of the water. On the ceiling, several large rattan paddle fans circulated air through the room, and the walls were decorated with colorful maritime-themed pastels and large three-dimensional replicas of lake fish.

Annie and Ed were seated at a small table against a window, and within seconds the server appeared. He introduced himself, recited the specials, handed them menus, and after confirming that they didn't need their beverages to be refilled, said he'd be back in a few minutes to take their orders.

"Annie, talk to me. What's bothering you?"

Annie took a deep breath. "I was hoping not to spoil our evening, but I've been obsessing for hours, so I might as well get it out. I'm upset with myself; I've been withholding information regarding the investigation. Not intentionally. I just forgot with all that's been going on. I feel horrible about it."

She swallowed, then continued. "I hadn't thought about it until today, but I may know who killed George, Ed. I just don't know why. It's hard for me to even say this, but I'm fearful it might be Jason. I called him the morning of the murder to talk about a brochure he's writing on the War of 1812. He said he was going to speak with Amanda and then visit the cemetery. The techs identified the tire tracks from his car, along with others. It's possible his and George's paths may have crossed."

"If that's true, Annie, it doesn't mean Jason's our killer," Ed responded.

She held up her hand. "Please, Ed, let me continue. I went into the museum later that morning on my way to the market to check the mail and answering machine and that's when I retrieved George's message.

"I'd closed the museum for the day and told Jason that after he finished his assignments he could go home. A few minutes later, he called me back and said that after his interview with Amanda he was going to come back to the office to compose his notes. His vehicle was parked in our lot, and I went upstairs to talk with him. I figured he must have visited the cemetery first, maybe the timing worked better for Amanda, and then he walked to her house to interview her. It may have taken longer than he expected, he wasn't at his desk. As I was leaving, I noticed a prescription on his desk.

"I know I shouldn't have done it, but I was curious and picked it up. It was a bottle of digitalis with his name on it. I had no idea he has a heart condition, Ed. He's young and seems fit. I was shocked; still, I'd snooped and felt uneasy questioning him about it and hoped he'd confide in me. He hasn't, and I forgot about it until this afternoon.

"As I said earlier, maybe his and George's paths crossed. He and George introduce themselves; George, trusting him, shows him what he discovered. Jason could have picked up the prescription before heading to the cemetery and still had it in his car. After determining the value of the artifact, he goes back to the car, gets a pill or two and slips it into George's tea."

The server returned, and the couple ordered their entrees and glasses of wine. The drinks arrived quickly, and after taking a sip of his Cabernet Sauvignon, Ed took Annie's hand and smiled at her. "First of all, you have no idea what George wanted to show you. It could have been a tombstone or the terrible state the cemetery was in. Jason had no idea when he visited the cemetery that George would be there unless he listened to the phone message, but the timing isn't right for him to have done that."

"It might have been an opportunistic crime, Ed. My instincts are telling me that George found some sort of artifact, maybe something worth a lot of money or with significant historical value," Annie insisted, sipping her Sauvignon Blanc. "I have no idea what Jason's financial situation is, but maybe he needs money."

"Annie, I simply can't imagine Jason murdering George to profit from something he found, it seems a bit of a stretch to me. Given the information I currently have, I'm going to explore other leads first."

Annie sighed. "Still, Ed, you have to admit that it's awfully strange that Jason is taking the same drug that killed George."

"It does seem odd, but there's also the possibility that it's completely coincidental. If he killed George, why would he leave the prescription in plain view instead of hiding it?"

"Because the temperature was rising, and he didn't want to leave it in a hot car. He probably never imagined I'd be in the office. I told him I was taking the day off, so he had no reason to hide the drug."

"Annie, I'm going to err on the side of caution and believe there's a reasonable explanation. Please don't obsess about this. I think you may be getting yourself overworked for no reason."

He continued, "Will Jason be in the office tomorrow?"

"Yes, about 10:00."

"Then I'll speak with him before I go into the city to interview George's co-workers. I'm hoping to get this wrapped up before we go to England in a few weeks."

"I hope so, too, Ed," Annie sighed. "I want to enjoy our trip without having to think about the murder."

As they were finishing their meal, a figure appeared behind Annie and bent down to give her a hug. She looked up to see Sheila Caldwell, a partner in the same law firm as Suzanne's boyfriend, Garrett Rosenfeld; and Sheila's spouse, Amy McBride, who was the pastry chef at Suzanne's parents' Caribbean restaurant, Callaloo. Annie had hoped to have an evening without interruptions. Despite that, she was pleased to see them.

Sheila smiled. "Hello, you two. What a surprise to see you here."

Annie jumped up to hug Sheila and Amy; then Ed stood and pulled them both into a hug.

"We needed a quiet dinner. You heard, I guess, about the murder of our friend, George Wright and that Ed is helping to investigate it?"

"We did," Sheila answered. "Suzanne was upset about the two of you finding the body and told Garrett, who, of course, mentioned it to me. Another murder in Lighthouse Cove, especially so recently after Emily's death, is quite shocking."

Ed responded, "Hopefully this one will be easier and quicker to solve. Annie and I are going to England in a few weeks." He explained the reason for their trip.

The four friends chatted for a few minutes; then Amy said to Sheila, "Perhaps we need to leave these two alone to finish their meal. And I'm starving."

A short while later, Ed paid the bill and he and Annie walked over to the piano and sat down in the comfortable, swivel bucket chairs surrounding it, enjoying for several minutes the American Songbook standards the piano player performed.

"I regret this evening didn't turn out to be as relaxing as we expected," Annie remarked.

"There will be other evenings. This was a discussion we needed to have."

A few hours later, after watching the evening news, Ed fell into a restless sleep, but Annie couldn't quiet her mind. She tossed and turned, thinking about Jason and started to cry, silently, she didn't want to wake Ed. After a few minutes she felt his hand on her shoulder.

"Annie, what's wrong?"

"Oh, Ed, I'm terribly sad. Here I am mentoring this young man, and he could be our murderer. His references and scholastic record are great. I thought he'd be a perfect fit for us. Maybe I was wrong."

"Annie, please don't do this to yourself. I promise I'll speak with Jason tomorrow, and we'll get to the bottom of this. I really believe that George's murder has nothing to do with him. Try and get some sleep."

From the Letters of Rebecca Fitzhugh

December,1815
My dear Marigold,

We are settled in the Pengelley home in Newfoundland, and both the captain and his wife have made us welcome and are delighted we shall be with them to celebrate the birth of our Savior and usher in the new year.

Mrs. Pengelley is a grandmotherly sort who showers Patience and Charity with love and attention. They are enjoying helping her bake, and she is teaching them to sew. They adore playing in the snow and accompanying their adopted grandmother to the market on snowshoes that the captain has crafted for them. I am teaching them to read.

Despite protestations from Mrs. Pengelley, I have taken on the responsibility of cooking the evening meal, a task I am enjoying immensely. She and the captain, who are childless, care for us as though we were their own, and my happiness is doubled by providing her with some respite at day's end.

Their cozy home is well-provisioned, and we have a glorious view of the harbor and beyond it the ocean with its choppy waves and frozen spray. Nicely is the real princess here, with a bed of her own near the hearth and plenty of warm milk to drink and fish to eat. At least for now, her mousing days are over!

Oh, and I have glorious news!! My dear Robert's parents have written to me, and God in his Glory, my husband still lives. His family, landowners and cousins of King George III, have successfully appealed to him to postpone the trial until the girls and I complete our journey. While dismayed my beloved and I shall not live happily together until old age, I take comfort that we shall see our dear father and husband once more, and we know he will die as a hero in his adopted country. I've been told his health is adequate and spirits good and that he has been informed of our journey.

I will write again, Marigold, but the weather may preclude your receiving any additional correspondence from me until spring.

As always, I send much love to you and Remington.
Rebecca

Chapter 22

Jason Shipley had a lot on his plate, and he was scared and anxious. Until recently, he felt like he had control of his life; now that had changed. Now it felt like his whole world was crumbling, and he didn't like it. He got good grades at school and had been happy working for Annie, nevertheless he didn't want to see her today. He didn't want to see anyone. He wanted to bury his head in the sand and pretend life was back to normal.

He wanted to turn back the clock to a time when life seemed simpler and was lots more fun. He feared he would never have fun again. His parents had advised him that life had its ups and downs, but the good times helped to strengthen people so they could deal with the down times. He wasn't sure. What had recently happened might affect his entire future, if he couldn't figure out how to deal with it.

He parked his old Honda Civic in the museum's parking lot at just before 10 a.m. The museum didn't open until 11:00 that day; an SUV he didn't recognize sat next to Annie's car. Maybe it was a vendor, or a volunteer Annie was meeting with before the museum filled with visitors.

Taking a deep breath, he let himself into the building and walked up the steps to his office, which was adjacent to the library on the second floor. It contained a desk, swivel chair, floor lamp, small bookcase and computer, along with two folding chairs for visitors.

The chairs were occupied by Annie and her husband, Ed.

Annie stood up. "Jason, this is my husband, Ed. I think the two of you met when you first started working here."

"Yes. I remember you, Mr. DeCleryk."

Annie continued. "Ed's been hired to investigate the murder of our dear friend, George Wright. He wants to ask you a few questions."

The wiry young man, wearing trim jeans and a yellow polo shirt, looked at Annie with guileless hazel eyes. "I heard about that awful murder. As you know, I was at the cemetery the day Mr. Wright died, but I didn't see anything," he volunteered, then looked at Ed. "I don't know what I could tell you that would help with the investigation, Mr. DeCleryk."

"Maybe you know more than you think, Jason. That's what Ed wants to talk with you about." Annie stood up and walked out of the room.

Ed noticed that the young man seemed tense. "Please call me Ed, Jason. There's no need for you to be nervous. It helps during an investigation to get different perspectives."

"Do I need a lawyer?" The young man seemed terrified.

"I can't imagine why you would, unless you've done something wrong. We're just trying to put the pieces together, and I'd appreciate your help. I'll ask a few questions, should you become uncomfortable at any time, we can stop."

He continued, "Please think hard about anything you may have noticed at the cemetery that morning."

Jason took a deep breath. "I drove there before I went to see Mrs. Reynolds; the timing worked better for her. The cemetery was a mess. There were bones scattered about; mud, debris, even pieces of caskets. I noticed footprints and animal prints, some brush had been cleared—that was it.

"I explored for several minutes, mainly trying to read the inscriptions on the headstones. They were dirty and worn. I decided I'd leave and come back some other time with paper and charcoal and do some rubbings that might help me identify names. It was just about time for my visit with Mrs. Reynolds. I drove back to the museum and parked. She doesn't live far, so after grabbing my notes for the interview from my desk, I walked to her house."

He smiled. "She's a sweet old lady," he volunteered. "She'd baked scones and served tea at a little table overlooking her garden. I got scads of information from her about her ancestor, Robert Fitzhugh, and how he was a hero in the War of 1812. We hit it off, and I promised I'd come back and visit again soon."

Ed believed him, yet he was puzzled about the to-go cup that had been discovered. "Did you happen to notice a to-go cup at the site?"

"No, I didn't," Jason admitted. "Why?"

"Just curious."

Ed thought, *This isn't making sense. Jason seems to be telling the truth. In that case, George, after leaving a message for Annie, must have left the site and returned with his truck and tools and the to-go cup of tea that had been spiked with the digitalis before he got there or possibly by someone who was at the site at the same time as he. If not Jason, then who?* He had one more question.

"Jason, Annie came up to your office between your visit to the cemetery and meeting with Amanda, and she noticed a prescription on your desk. She hoped you'd confide in her if you're having health problems. I'm certain she'd have no issue with your taking time off to deal with a medical condition."

Jason looked confused. "The prescription isn't mine; it's for my dad. I'm Jason K., for Keith; the name on the prescription is for Jason C. Shipley, the *C* stands for Charles." Ed seemed like a sympathetic person; the young man confided in him.

His father, in his late 40s, had recently suffered a serious heart attack. He'd survived but was placed on disability, and the doctors weren't sure when he'd be able to return to his job as a chemist at Bausch and Lomb. Jason had recently learned that the condition was congenital.

His grandfather, whom he'd never known, had died in his 40s as had his great-grandfather. The young man, close to his father, was terrified not only of losing him but also concerned about his own health as he got older. To add to his stress, he worried about the family's finances and was not sure he'd be able to stay in school.

"I've been trying to take some pressure off my mom. She works part-time at a travel agency, but what she makes isn't nearly enough to support us. I offered to quit school and get a full-time job; she was adamant we didn't need for me to do that. She explained that my dad's disability policy is excellent, plus we have enough savings to get us through hard times. She was thinking about working full-time before this happened and said we needed to concentrate on my dad getting strong again and for me to finish college.

"She has a lot on her plate. She mentioned she was going to pick up my dad's prescription after a meeting she'd scheduled at the agency to ask about starting a full-time position. I offered to do it. After I picked it up, I drove over here. It was already in the 70s, and I didn't want to leave it in a hot car so brought it up to the office."

Ed believed Jason and knew he could easily verify his story. This young man was not George's murderer.

He stood up and put his hand out. "Thank you for taking time to talk with me, Jason. You've helped a lot with the sequence of events that day.

"May I tell Annie about what's going on with your family or will you do it? I think she'd like to know."

"Thanks for offering, but I'll tell her."

"I'm sorry for your troubles and know she will be, too, and I truly hope your dad recovers. Annie has been pleased with your work; I expect that's at least one thing you won't have to worry about. It sounds as though your parents have a plan that will keep the family afloat for the time being. From experience I know that sometimes you just have to trust that things will work out."

Jason shook Ed's hand with a firm grip. After Ed left, he put his hands over his face and cried for a few minutes, both with relief and sadness. Then he went to his computer and continued writing the brochure on the War of 1812.

Chapter 23

Ed and Annie awoke to a day that befitted the occasion. Layers of clouds the color of pewter rimmed the sky forecasting impending rain and a cool front. The stormy steel-wool lake churned and roiled, spewing cold, white spray high onto the rocks at the base of their bluff. George Wright's memorial service later that morning would be partly a celebration of his life, but also a grieving theatre of those who mourned his too-early death.

After eating a light breakfast and walking Gretchen, who sensing something was awry was remarkably subdued, the pair showered and dressed in somber dark clothing. They had decided to walk the two blocks to the nondenominational Peace Church, carrying umbrellas should the rain descend earlier than anticipated.

Carrie was waiting in the church lobby with Ed's Navy buddies and their spouses and significant others when Ed and Annie arrived. Everyone hugged and they entered the sanctuary as a group, sitting in the second row on the left, behind Sally Wright, her daughter and family, and George's parents. Across the aisle, Sally's siblings and their families sat with Eric's parents, and behind them George's co-workers. The clouds had thickened, and no sunlight streamed through the stained-glass windows that lined the walls with pastoral, calming scenes.

The service honored the death of the retired military officer. Family members gave emotional eulogies, the minister encouraged those present to continue to offer support and love to George's family and finished with a homily about forgiveness.

Per Sally's request, no volley was fired. At the appointed time, a Navy ensign, attired in military dress, walked down the aisle playing *Taps*. Two other Navy officers walked to the front of the church with an American flag.

In normal circumstances the flag was placed on the coffin; since George had been cremated, they unfolded and then refolded it, a symbolic gesture, and passed it off to Ed. Representing the SEALs, Ed came forward, kneeled in front of Sally and after kissing her gently on the cheek, presented her with the flag, her family and friends weeping softly. A catered luncheon at Windy Bluff followed the service.

Later that afternoon, Ed and Annie nursed glasses of wine as they sat quietly and rocked on matching rockers on their back porch. The clouds that had formed that morning now cried forth a steady, gentle rain and a few waves lapped somberly onto the shore, appearing weary from their earlier agitation. Even the gulls were quiet. It was as though the entire village were in mourning.

"It's not surprising we're getting rain," Annie remarked. "Not that we need it, but it's a fitting end to a sad, sad day. How are you holding up?"

"Not well. I can't begin to tell you how difficult it was for me to hand Sally the flag."

"I could see you were struggling to contain your tears, Ed. It would have been okay to cry, everyone else was."

"I know, but I thought if I started, I'd not be able to control myself." He paused. "How's Sally?"

"It's hard to lose a loved one, Ed, especially under these circumstances. She's emotionally quite fragile and needs our support. I assured her that I'd keep in touch, and we would continue to include her in social activities. I'll make sure the rest of our friends do the same. As much as that will hopefully help, I can't imagine she'll ever fully recover from knowing her healthy, vital husband was murdered. I know I wouldn't."

The pair reminisced for several minutes about the happy times they'd had with George and Sally. Annie was upset to observe George's parents, who, increasingly frail, appeared pale and distraught at the funeral. George's mother had wept silently into a linen handkerchief, while his father had remained stoic.

At the reception, Lily had reported to Annie that for now the ongoing care at their cottage would continue, but she had begun researching continuing care facilities for her grandparents. She believed it was only a matter of months until that occurred.

She had confessed that she continued to feel guilty about not including George in the day trip she'd taken with her mother to Skaneateles. Despite being reassured that her father's death was not her fault, she was struggling. Annie convinced her to seek professional help and gave her the name of a friend who was a therapist in Rochester.

Ed took a sip of his wine. "Annie, I'm going to interview George's co-workers at Barrow and Croft at 10 tomorrow morning. My first interview is with Monica Snyder, the managing partner. She may know of any disgruntled employees or clients who may have wanted to harm him.

"I spoke briefly with Averill at the reception. He mentioned another retired SEAL, Peter Rigby, who works for that firm. He suggested I might also want to interview him. Averill volunteered that Peter and his wife, Laura, were friends with George and Sally; he and

Liz had met them one evening at George and Sally's home. Laura was at the funeral and the reception; because of a family emergency, Peter was unable to attend. I have a lot to think about and don't want to forget anything. I'm going to go into my study and make some notes."

"How long will that take, Ed? I'd like to take a walk in the rain before dinner. Perhaps we can do something low-key tonight like reading or watching a show on PBS."

Ed sighed. "It won't take long. Give me half-an-hour, and I'll join you."

Chapter 24

The gentle rain continued throughout the night but had stopped before dawn, and the clouds had given way to bright sun. Ed headed out the door at 9:00 a.m. in order to get to his interview with Monica Snyder at 10:00. He wanted to give himself ample time; one could never quite predict the traffic on Route 104 or the Rochester Beltway.

The water was sparkling on Irondequoit Bay. He noticed several sailboats out for an early, lazy sail, and in the distance, the broad, blue expanse of Lake Ontario as he crossed over the Bay Bridge. He was feeling calmer than he had in days when his phone rang, startling him out of a peaceful reverie. He didn't recognize the phone number. Switching the phone to Blue Tooth, he answered. "Hello. This is Ed Decleryk."

"Mr. DeCleryk, this is Abby Baker. I'm Monica Snyder's administrative assistant. She asked me to call to let you know she's in a meeting that's taking longer than expected and would like to reschedule to 11:00. If you're on your way, I can meet you in the lobby and escort you to a lounge where you can have coffee and wait for her. Or, we can postpone until later this afternoon or tomorrow if that works better for you."

While Ed understood that circumstances change, he was eager to get the interview over with. "I left Lighthouse Cove at about 9:00, Abby, to give myself extra time in case I got caught up in rush hour traffic. Thanks for the offer, but I'll see Ms. Snyder at 11:00. I have a couple things I can do in the meantime. I appreciate the call."

After hanging up, Ed decided to drive to Park Street, which was a few blocks from the financial services' office, for coffee and a pastry at Park Street Bakery and Café. It was located next door to Gallery 21, an art and sculpture gallery owned by his friend, Jon Bradford. He found a parking space a half block away, walked to the Café and ordered a bear claw and black coffee, and for several minutes perused his notes. He still had time before his appointment and headed to the gallery, hoping to visit with Jon.

He entered the Federal-style red brick building that sat hip-to-hip with its neighbors on each side, and Sophie, Jon's niece and receptionist, rose from her desk to greet him with a big hug, smiling broadly. Her gorgeous red hair cascaded down her back, and today the tall, green-eyed beauty was wearing an emerald green tunic top; black, cropped leggings and short black booties. She flashed her hand at Ed.

"Hunter and I just got engaged. Isn't that wonderful?" Sophie and her fiancé, graduates of the Eastman School of Music, performed in a chamber music quartet at night.

"Congratulations!" Ed exclaimed, admiring the ring.

Just then, Jon Bradford stepped out of his office. When he saw Ed, the tall, striking dark haired man grinned, walked over and hugged him.

"It's great to see you, Ed. It's been way too long."

"I know, Jon. I guess life gets in the way sometimes. How are you?"

Before responding, Jon remarked, "I heard about the murder in Lighthouse Cove. That's tough, especially so soon after Emily's murder. What brings you here?"

"I have an appointment with the managing partner of the financial services company where George worked but had some time on my hands so decided to drop by to see how you're a doing."

"I will forever miss Emily and still can't wrap my head around why she was senselessly murdered. I've learned that time does heal and I'm doing much better. I've started dating again."

"That's wonderful news! Anyone special?"

"Yes. Remember when you interviewed me after Emily died that I told you I'd been in Buffalo the night before to talk with an up-and-coming glass sculptor about exhibiting here?"

"I do," Ed responded.

"Her name is Stephanie Morris." He pointed to a stunning, colorful glass bowl that stood on a black enameled pedestal in a corner. "That's one of hers. Her work is incredible, as is she. Emily would have liked her."

"You have an open invitation to visit Annie and me anytime that works for the two of you. We'd love to meet her."

"I'll eventually do that; it just may not be for several months. Stephanie is still living in Buffalo, and we're taking this slowly."

The three friends chatted amiably for a few more minutes until it was time for Ed to leave for his appointment. He reiterated that he hoped Jon would keep in touch.

Chapter 25

While Ed was in Rochester, Annie called her friend
Amanda to check on her and invite her to speak at the
history talk she was planning for the fall.

"I'm so happy you called, dear."

"I was wondering how you're doing, Amanda. I've
been negligent in keeping in touch lately, and I feel
awful about it."

"I know, dear, but please don't fret. I assume you
and your handsome husband have been busy; I heard
about that horrible murder in the old cemetery. Do you
think Mr. Wright's death is related to what he was
doing there, or was it just a coincidence and he was at
the wrong place at the wrong time?"

"No one knows yet. Ed's investigating the murder
and looking at all possibilities."

"I hope the killer is apprehended soon; it's quite
frightening to think that someone like that is lurking
about in our community," Amanda replied.

Annie, segueing to the second reason for her call,
was pleased when her friend agreed to speak at the fall
event and indicated that she'd be back in touch a few
days before the event to arrange for transportation.

As they were concluding their conversation, Amanda
volunteered how she'd enjoyed spending time with
Jason Shipley the day he interviewed her.

"He's a nice young man. All I could offer him were
scones and tea, and it was getting close to lunch time. I
hadn't thought about the timing of it. He seemed to like
the scones, and I fixed up an herbal tea for him that

came from peppermint, hyssop and chamomile herbs I'd dried last year from my garden. I hope he visits again."

Annie responded that Jason had also enjoyed spending time with Amanda and had indicated that he'd return for a visit soon. Plus, he'd want her to read the brochure he was writing to make sure that the facts about Robert Fitzhugh were accurate.

Chapter 26

Ed arrived at the financial services firm a few minutes before 11:00 and was ushered into Monica Snyder's office, which was located on the top floor of a building in Rochester overlooking High Falls. It was decorated with lots of chrome, leather and glass. A few professional certificates and trendy, modern artwork hung on the walls.

No photos of family members or pets were on her desk, and the only reading materials were journals, newspapers and business periodicals. The stylish, reed-thin woman, who appeared to be in her mid-40s, shook Ed's hand with a firm grip. He recognized her from George's memorial service. She apologized for the delay.

"I had a conference call that lasted much longer than I expected and appreciate your flexibility. I understand you wish to speak with me about George Wright's murder; I don't know what I can tell you that will help with your investigation. I keep a pretty close eye on things here, and there's no animosity among any of our employees that I'm aware of."

"I appreciate that, Ms. Snyder. It appears I won't need to interview them, but there's one other person I'd like to speak with who's a retired SEAL."

"You must mean Peter Rigby." Monica pursed her lips. "He was out of the office for several days dealing with a family emergency before George died and didn't return until after the funeral. I can assure you he didn't kill George; they were close friends."

Ed replied, "He's not a suspect, and I'm sorry you thought I was implying that he was. I'm aware that the two men were friends, and I'm curious about whether George might have confided in him about threats against his life that he was unable to talk about to Sally."

"Sorry if I appeared defensive, Mr. DeCleryk. Since George's murder, I've been a bit on edge. Peter's here today; I can ask him to join us." She reached for the buzzer on her phone.

"That's not necessary. It seems like you're very busy, and I can interview him in his office after you and I are finished here."

"Thank you. Is there anything else I can help you with?

"Yes. You said you're positive no employees would have been involved in George's death, but what about his clients?"

"I'm also not aware of any clients who would have harbored animosity against George. I wouldn't recommend your trying to interview all of them; I can assure you it would be a waste of your time. If you decide to go in that direction, please understand that unless you serve me with a subpoena, I won't be able to divulge any personal information about our clients. Our records are confidential."

"I understand you're obligated by law to protect your clients' privacy, but certainly you must understand my need to look at every angle to solve the case," Ed responded patiently.

Monica relaxed. "I'm sorry to be appearing so difficult, but I hope you can understand my dilemma. We have weekly meetings here in the office, and—trust me on this—there haven't ever been any reports of clients who might wish to harm any of our employees, including George."

Ed sighed. "While I was hoping for a different outcome, I agree that it's probably not in either of our best interests to get a subpoena for the list of all of George's clients. It's just that I'm very frustrated by not being able to narrow down who might have killed George."

"Mr. DeCleryk, I liked George. He was a fine man and good at his job. But I have absolute faith that no one here in the office or any of George's clients would have wanted him dead."

Ed thanked her for cooperating. Glancing at her watch again, the woman said she had another meeting, and Abby would escort him to Peter Rigby's office.

Rigby was a small, smartly dressed man with short cropped blond hair, blue eyes and high cheekbones. He had a firm handshake, looked Ed directly in the eye, and expressed his sadness at George's death and regret he'd be unable to attend his funeral. He verified that he'd been a SEAL, many years after George had been in the service; he'd never been under his command. He genuinely liked the man, they worked companionably together, and despite their age differences had bonded and socialized together with their wives. Like Monica, he was unaware of any recent threats to George's life that Sally wouldn't have known about; the couple didn't keep secrets, and he believed if she knew something, she would've been forthcoming to it about Ed.

Ed was bone tired, and for a moment he fleetingly thought that agreeing to investigate George's murder had been, perhaps, a mistake. He had too much emotionally invested in finding his friend's killer, and it was taking its toll on him.

He had eagerly accepted Carrie's offer; but now he was doubting his decision. Perhaps he should have declined and let her hire someone else who didn't care as much about George and his family. He acknowledged that despite his feelings, he couldn't quit now; he was too far into the investigation, but decided his interview with George's parents could wait until tomorrow.

Back in his car, he called Carrie and gave her a summary of his meetings with Monica Snyder and Peter Rigby.

He'd had a frustrating morning and decided he'd done enough for today and would go home, take Gretchen for a walk, and work on one of his projects. And he needed to think. He still believed someone had information that could help him solve the case.

Chapter 27

George's killer was smiling. It had all been quite easy, and no one would possibly suspect who had done the deed. The issue had been resolved; mission accomplished, the motive would never be discovered. Poison was such an appropriate way to rid the world of undesirables.

Taking another life was just part of the process— that was that. When opportunity strikes, one must take advantage of it. Awful for the victim's family, still, lots of folks experienced loss, and this one, from all accounts, had lived to almost old age. Some died young through no fault of their own; this victim had been luckier than many.

The killer turned on the radio to a station playing lovely, soothing, classical music, and decided to spend the afternoon reading something light and entertaining. Agatha Christie's Appointment with Death *seemed appropriate and was pulled from the shelf. The killer laughed. It was especially fitting given how the victim was murdered—both inspirational and illuminating.*

Today would be a reading day, although there was still more to be done to continue to protect and preserve. But that could wait.

Yes, the issue had been resolved. At least for the time being.

Chapter 28

The next morning, after breakfasting with Annie and walking Gretchen, Ed dialed the phone number at Averill and Liz Wright's cottage. The retired engineer answered and sounded weak but eager to talk with Ed and said he could meet with him at 11:00. Liz would not be joining them. She was terribly depressed, would neither eat nor drink and lay in bed staring at the ceiling. Averill was terrified she would die of grief before the month was out.

Ed decided to call Suzanne, who had a background in mental health, after the interview. She might be able to recommend a counselor who could help the elderly couple deal with their grief. He didn't want to impose on Sally who, while fond of her in-laws, was in no condition to provide them with emotional support.

The couple, both in their late 80s, lived in a small, one-story cottage on Third Street with views of the lake. Built in the 1940s, it had been remodeled and upgraded but still retained some of its original character.

Using a cane, Averill Wright opened the front door and ushered Ed inside. He was dressed in gray pants, a white button-down shirt, and a blue sports coat. In all the years Ed had known him, the retired engineer had always been impeccably dressed. He had aged in the past several days and was noticeably frail, with a slight tremor to his papery, spotted hands.

"Liz, my dear, Ed DeCleryk is here." Averill called out to his wife. "Won't you please say hello to him?"

She didn't answer; he shook his head. "Our caregiver is with her now; she's a compassionate and kind woman. I was hoping she'd be able to convince my wife to get out of bed, but nothing seems to be working."

Ed feared that neither of the couple would live much longer, given the trauma of losing their only child.

Averill offered Ed a drink—coffee, tea or water—which he declined. Then after accepting Ed's condolences, he motioned for him to sit on the flowered sofa that had been placed along a wall in the living room across from two matching chairs. The room was light-filled and pleasant, with antiques, a fireplace with a stone hearth and mantel, and lots of photos of the Wright family.

"My heart is broken, Ed. I can't imagine who would want to kill George. I'm not sure that Liz nor I will survive this blow."

Ed expressed sympathy and admitted his own grief. The two men chatted for a few minutes before Ed began the interview.

"I know how hard this is for you, Averill, but you and George were close. Can you remember anything in past or recent conversations that would lead you to believe someone was threatening him?"

Averill thought for a moment." No, nothing." Then his eyes widened as something occurred to him.

"Maybe," he responded. "I hadn't thought about it until just now; it was long ago, and I can't imagine it would have anything to do with George's death. I'm not even sure that what I thought I overheard was accurate."

Ed looked at Averill quizzically. "Averill?"

The older man reminded Ed that after retiring from the Air Force, George had moved to Boston with his family to begin studying for a Masters' degree at the Carroll School of Finance at Boston College. He had also obtained a fellowship that required him to teach a class three nights a week.

Averill recalled that during the family's second year in Boston, he and Liz had visited them during spring break. One afternoon Liz, Sally and Lily went out for lunch and then to visit some museums while George and Averill stayed at home to watch a ball game in the living room. During the third inning, George's cell phone, that was sitting on an end table next to him, rang. He looked at the caller ID, picked it up, answered it, and walked into his study to continue the conversation.

"I heard him thanking the caller for returning his call. I assumed it had to do with his classes and didn't think much about it. I'd been drinking coffee and wanted to refill my cup and had to pass the study to get to the kitchen. I heard George say something that sounded like, 'death threat, pull cuff' and 'CIA'."

"Did you ask about it?"

"No, not at first. I was alarmed but didn't want him to think I was eavesdropping. I went to the kitchen, got my coffee and then walked back to the living room before George ended the conversation. I concentrated on the TV and shortly after, George returned from his study. I waited until the game ended and then admitted I'd overheard his conversation and was concerned that his life was being threatened."

"What was his response?"

George laughed, Averill replied, and reminded his father that the family had been encouraging him to be tested for hearing loss. "He assured me that I'd completely misheard the conversation and that I needed to seriously consider getting hearing aids."

"Did he say what the conversation was about?"

Averill reported that George had sheepishly confessed that what his father had overheard was a conversation between himself and one of Sally's friends about a gift he wanted to surprise her with.

"Sally, after spending an afternoon shopping with the friend, had confessed to George that she'd found the perfect dress for the college faculty's Spring Ball. She didn't purchase it; she thought it was too expensive.

"She was disappointed; she loved the dress. George decided to buy it as a surprise but couldn't remember the name of the store. He called and left a message for her friend who called back that afternoon and gave him the name of the boutique, Dress Threads. George repeated it and said he hoped he could 'pull it off' and then ended the conversation with 'see ya'."

"Did you believe him?"

"No. Something about his response and the way he looked at me lacked credibility, but I had no idea why he would lie. I was concerned."

"Did you think to check for a boutique with that name to see if your suspicions were correct?" Ed asked.

"No. That would have meant I mistrusted my son, and he'd never given me any reason to believe he was a liar. I decided to let it drop; perhaps I *had* misheard the conversation. I felt guilty that I'd doubted my son."

Averill continued, "After George finished his degree, as you know, he was hired as a financial adviser with Barrow and Croft. I'm not aware of any threats to his life since they moved back to the area, although he wouldn't have necessarily confided in me. Now I'm wondering if what I heard was correct. Maybe he had ties to the CIA, someone *had* threatened to kill him and for whatever reason had bided his time. It seems farfetched, I know, but still it might be worth checking out."

Ed agreed. He had a contact, Samir Abadi, who had been a SEAL under his command and after retiring from the service had eventually become an analyst for the CIA. Before he left, Ed hugged Averill, expressed concern for Liz and promised to call after he spoke with his friend.

Chapter 29

Ed, now back at home, called Suzanne. She'd just finished teaching a yoga class and was taking a break before her class on nutrition for better health started.

After hearing about George's parents, she promised to contact the county office on aging. "They have grief counselors, Ed, plus they can provide help with any of their other needs. I'll ask that they plan a visit as soon as possible."

After ending the call, Ed changed into a pair of shorts and a golf shirt and went into his study with a glass of iced tea to plan his next steps. Gretchen, after greeting him in her usual, boisterous way, settled down at his feet and promptly fell asleep. He smiled, and feeling comforted by her warm body against his legs, reached down to stroke her velvety ears.

Annie would be returning home in a little while, and they would enjoy their nightly tradition of drinks and conversation before dinner on the back patio. He picked up the phone and dialed Samir's number. The call went to voice mail, and Ed left a short message asking his friend to call him back at his earliest convenience. Then he resolved that for tonight he was going to put aside the investigation.

He had just dozed off in his leather recliner but awoke, startled, as he heard Annie announce, "Ed, I'm home." Pulling himself up from a slump, he stood up and stretched as she walked into the room.

"How was your day?" Annie asked as she reached up to kiss him.

"Not easy, Let's talk about it over drinks. And you?"

"I had a good day. Jason is making progress on the brochures; I scheduled the speakers for our History Alive series, and we have all the sponsors' checks for our summer Concerts on the Bluff."

Ed smiled and hugged her, and the couple repaired to the back porch with a bottle of wine and a plate of cheese and crackers. He summarized his interviews with Monica Snyder and Peter Rigby at George's firm, his conversation with George's father and his call to his friend at the CIA. He was doubtful that the conversation would be productive, nevertheless he felt obligated to follow up on the lead.

"I'm hoping Samir will have the authority to tell me if he knows whether George had been involved with the CIA like Averill suspects and, if so, if he was aware of any threats on his life."

"Sally told Carrie and me on the day he died that she and George had no secrets, Ed. But maybe that's not true. If he was working for the CIA would he have been able to share that with her? Is that even possible?"

"I think it would depend on the type of position he had. Not every CIA employee is a spy, Annie. I'm positive that George would never have done anything to put his family in harm's way; he loved them too much.

"This could be another false lead, or maybe Samir won't get clearance to speak with me about it. In that case, I'm just not sure how I'm going to proceed. I was hoping to solve the case before we leave for our trip."

"Ed, in the end it will work out. We'll go to England and have a wonderful time. Speaking of trips, how would you feel about going away this weekend? It might be nice for us to get out of town for a couple days."

"Where would you like to go?"

"How about a trip to Gananoque? It's a short drive, and I found a lovely inn that's located right on the St. Lawrence River. I've heard it has a terrific spa and two excellent restaurants. I've already called Sandy, and she'll watch Gretchen for us."

"I'd like to do that, Annie, depending on what I find out from Samir. I may need to make a trip to D.C.to meet with him. You're welcome to come with me; in fact, I could use the company. We can break up the trip and stop in Baltimore on the way down and spend the night at Inner Harbor."

"That sounds like fun, Ed, and when we're in Washington, I can visit some museums while the two of you are meeting. But it's a long drive, and I'm hoping you'll get the information you need on the phone. Then we can take the weekend off to do something completely recreational."

After a few more minutes, Annie went inside to bring dinner out. She had prepared Tuna Nicoise and served it with a crusty loaf of bread. After cleaning up, the couple moved into the living room, where they spent the evening reading and doing crossword puzzles. Then they went to bed.

Chapter 30

A light rain had fallen overnight, and the day was chilly, although weather often turned cooler toward the end of May. Ed told Annie that since he hadn't yet heard back from his friend, to go ahead and plan the trip to Gananoque.

Over breakfast, Annie suggested they stop for lunch in Sackets Harbor on their way to Canada. Located on Lake Ontario within proximity to the St. Lawrence River, the historic village had been occupied by the U.S. Navy during the War of 1812.

Two small, decisive battles had been fought on land facing the harbor that had since been preserved for visitors, and an adjacent armory had been converted into a museum with war memorabilia, historical posters, a library and bookstore.

"Ed, we've been to Sackets Harbor many times, but we've never explored the battlefield or armory. This time I'd like to do that. I might learn something I can pass on to Jason for his project."

He suggested, "Or, we can go to Gananoque some other time and stay in Sackets Harbor instead. I expect this time of year we'd have no trouble finding an inn or B&B there."

"I'd like to proceed with our original plan. There's a boat tour on the Canadian side of the Thousand Islands that leaves from the dock just outside the inn. I expect it will be relaxing, and the scenery is beautiful."

As the pair was putting their dishes into the dishwasher, Ed's phone rang. It was Samir Abadi. "Hi,

Samir. Thanks for getting back to me." Ed gave his friend the details of George's murder and his conversation with Averill Wright.

The CIA officer was uncharacteristically quiet. Then he answered, "Give me a little time to do some research and I'll get back to you. I'm an officer, not an agent, so I'm not always up to speed when it comes to things like this. It may take a week or two."

Samir paused for a beat, then asked Ed if he'd retained his security clearance after leaving the SEALs. Ed replied that he'd let it lapse while working in law enforcement in Syracuse and as police chief of Lighthouse Cove, but had reapplied and been reinstated prior to becoming a criminal consultant.

"I consult with government defense contractors and law enforcement agencies, so it was imperative that I got my security clearance back. I'll scan and email the certificate to you."

"Thanks; that will help. I have nothing to share right now, but I'll call you back one way or another."

After ending the call, Ed turned to Annie and told her about his conversation with Samir. "He promised he'd get back to me after he receives my clearance certificate. Let's move forward with our weekend plans. I'll call Carrie with an update."

Chapter 31

"Hi, Carrie, how are you?" Ed asked.

"Better, Ed. I'm not as nauseous as I was a week ago; despite my best intentions, I'm eating like a pig and gained three pounds last week. We told our parents; they're delighted. My mother is positive that this time we'll have a boy. She says when she was pregnant with my brother, she had some of the same early symptoms."

She sighed. "We want a healthy child and don't care about the gender, but they're all hoping we'll have what they call, 'the million-dollar family'—that's supposedly a term for families with one of each. Whatever.... What's up?"

Ed briefed her on his interviews with Averill and Samir. "Samir appears to need my security clearance to talk with me and promised to call me back after he receives it. I'm hoping he'll have information that could help us solve the case; at this point I have no idea what that would be."

Ed apprised Carrie of his and Annie's planned weekend trip to Canada. "She thinks the trip will be relaxing and we need a change of scenery, and I agree, although I'm not sure I'll be able to get my mind off the case regardless. Don't hesitate to call me with updates."

"Ed, enjoy the weekend. Unless something breaks— and I doubt that—I'm not going to call you."

"I appreciate your sensitivity, Carrie. With George's murderer still at large, I'm not going to fully relax. Call me anytime."

That evening Ed and Annie met their friends Eve and Henri Beauvoir at The Brewery for drinks and dinner. They had hoped to eat outside on the deck, but the rain had continued as had the chilly temperatures. After being seated at a table with a view of the water, the friends were quickly served their beverages and then, several minutes later, their meals.

Fortunately, it was a quiet night, no entertainment had been planned and the weather seemed to keep patrons away. The couples were able to enjoy a quiet, uninterrupted dinner, and Ed and Annie felt more relaxed than they had in days. That night they slept soundly and dreamlessly.

Chapter 32

The rain had stopped overnight, and the birds, delighted with the change in weather, sang their morning songs in a raucous chorus that awakened Ed and Annie at 6:00 a.m. Unable to get back to sleep, the pair went downstairs. Ed let Gretchen out while Annie prepared their morning beverages.

They dropped Gretchen off at their pet sitter's house at 8:30 and headed east, stopping for breakfast in Fair Haven at a repurposed hardware store, the Nuts and Bolts Café, before continuing their journey to Sackets Harbor.

Deciding to take the scenic route, they drove along backroads with splendid vistas of dairy farms and fruit orchards and, as they approached the historic village, the eastern end of Lake Ontario as it spilled into the St. Lawrence River. They arrived at their destination just before noon.

The day was warm, and they chose to shop and visit the battlefield before having lunch. They purchased scented candles at a candle shop, and Ed sat on an upholstered chair reading tourist magazines, while Annie tried on a couple of tops at one of the boutiques, settling on a teal, sequin-encrusted tunic she'd wear for dinner that night along with skinny black pants and silver sandals.

A quick tour of the battlefield elicited no new information about the war, and the pair wandered into the museum. The converted armory contained exhibits, artifacts, a library and gift shop that contained books and brochures with tourist information. Annie carefully picked through a pile of old, dusty books on a discount table and found one entitled *The History of the War of 1812,* written by Morgan Lewis several years after the war had ended.

"Look at this, Ed." Annie walked over to her husband who was viewing an exhibit of muskets. "Lewis was Quartermaster General for Western New York during that war; Robert Fitzhugh was his cousin and a trusted aide. It might give us additional information for the brochure Jason is writing."

"Are you going to purchase a copy for Amanda? She might be interested in reading it."

"I can't. I talked with the docent, and this is the last copy; it's not an original, just a facsimile. The book is out of print. I expect Amanda has already read it and may have used it as resource for her own book; if not, she's welcome to borrow it after I read it. Since it's not an original copy, it won't be appropriate for me to add it to our exhibits, but at some point, I'll add it to our library."

After a leisurely lunch at Pier House, a restaurant that sat on a small promontory with views of the harbor, lake, and in the distance, Canada, the couple returned to their car and headed to Gananoque.

Ed's phone rang just as they had passed through customs. It was Carrie. Apologizing for the intrusion, she explained that she wanted to give him an update on her inquiries to law enforcement agencies around the lake. He remembered she'd spoken with them briefly after George's murder and at that time they'd indicated that nothing untoward had happened that would help to solve the case.

She indicated that recent reports of suspicious deaths and illnesses by poisoning were unrelated to George's murder. A woman had been killed after her husband laced her beer with rat poisoning, a child had gotten into his parents' medicine cabinet and ingested some pills in a container that was not child-proofed, fortunately the father had discovered what had happened and the child had lived.

One man had purposely swallowed an herbicide to commit suicide and another had overdosed on a mixture of cocaine and crystal meth, believing, according to his girlfriend, that he was just snorting cocaine.

"Thanks, Carrie. George's death appears to have been an isolated incident and not part of a larger pattern. We'll just have to figure out what's next once Annie and I get back from our trip."

Carrie apologized again for interrupting them, reiterated that she hoped Ed and Annie would have a relaxing and much-deserved weekend away, and Ed ended the call.

From the Letters of Rebecca Fitzhugh

April,1816
My dear Marigold,

Winter is behind us and spring has arrived, and what a glorious spring it is. We are preparing for the last part of our journey, and I can barely contain my joy that within several weeks we shall see Robert again. Charity and Patience continue to flourish, but to my dismay they rarely speak of their father and are sad to leave Mrs. Pengelley, who has been weeping for days in anticipation of our departure. Captain Pengelley has promised, once we are settled in England, to bring her to visit on one of his sojourns, although I fear it will be years before we see either of them after we disembark.

I have received one more letter from Robert's parents which contains a note from him; he sends his love and concern. They have arranged for their servants to meet us at the Port of London; one or both of my in-laws will also be there to greet us. They say Robert, despite his circumstances, is hale and hearty. I have begun to hope that now the War has ended he may be pardoned, especially as the months go by and a trial has not yet been scheduled. I know my thinking is fanciful and that his life may soon come to an end. The blessing will be to view his countenance one last time.

Robert's parents have determined that we shall settle with them rather than return to Lighthouse Cove after Robert's trial and sentencing. I am thinking on it yet have not determined where our place shall be. On one hand, I would be contented to be with those who have loved my husband since his birth; on the other hand, I do miss Lighthouse Cove and you and Remington. I have resolved to postpone a decision until I meet the Fitzhughs and can determine their true natures.

Yet again, my dear sister, I trust you and Remington are well and that the apple trees will bloom this year again in profusion.

With love,
Rebecca

Chapter 33

Ed and Annie checked in at the Gananoque Inn at
3:00, made 8:00 dinner reservations at Harborview
Restaurant, unpacked their suitcase and took a walk
through the charming riverside town, admiring the
stately Painted Lady Victorian homes that sat on tree-
lined streets. They stopped at the boat dock and booked
a tour of the 1,000 Islands for the next morning; then
returned to the inn in time for their 5:00 massages at the
spa. Now, fully relaxed, they headed to their room to
relax before dinner.

Ed fell promptly asleep on the bed while Annie sat
in a comfy chair facing the water and riffled through the
book she had purchased. As the docent had cautioned, it
looked like it was going to be an unexciting read and
she thought, *I don't have the patience for this right
now, I may not even add it to our library collection. It
looks awfully academic, and other than Amanda, unless
she's already read it, or maybe Jason, I can't imagine
anyone else being interested in it. Perhaps I'll read it
another time; maybe not until things settle down in the
fall.* She placed the book back in the bag, decided that
for now she'd had enough. Joining Ed on the bed, she
closed her eyes. A short nap before dinner would be
much more pleasurable.

The restaurant, located at the eastern end of the inn,
had windows facing the river and a large, ornately
carved oak fireplace that tonight was burning with a
small fire as the evening had become chilly. The tables,

set with white tablecloths, gleamed with sparkling crystal wine glasses, silver place settings and simple white dishware. Simple but elegant centerpieces consisted of colorful spring flowers placed in blue and white Delft vases. The room was lit with a trio of crystal chandeliers, the prisms capturing the light from the fireplace.

The sommelier presented them with the wine list, and the pair ordered a bottle of an Ontario Province Cabernet Sauvignon with a 92-point rating from *Wine Spectator*. A few minutes later, a waiter presented them with menus, recited the daily specials, then after their wine arrived, reappeared and took their orders.

While waiting for their salads, the couple sipped their wine and helped themselves to freshly baked crusty bread and melted brie. "I started reading the book I bought today," Annie mentioned to Ed.

"What's the verdict?" he asked.

"It's boring, and I'm not going to continue, at least not now. Jason might want to read it, but he can make that decision, I won't press it. He should have enough information from his other research, his discussion with Amanda and from reading the book she wrote."

"What about Amanda?"

"At some point if the topic comes up, I'll offer it to her, but I expect she's already read it and may have used it as a source for her own book. It must have taken her weeks to plough through it."

The salads came, and after that the entrees, which they both thoroughly enjoyed. Annie was way too full for dessert, but Ed ordered his favorite, Crème Brulee, along with a double espresso. Annie laughed.

"I have an iced tea at four o'clock in the afternoon and have trouble sleeping from the caffeine. You, on the other hand, have strong coffee at ten p.m. and will sleep like a baby. I don't know how you do it."

Ed grinned. "I'm a big, macho guy," he teased. "I can handle anything." He flexed a muscle. "And you're just a little thing." Annie laughed and rolled her eyes.

After signing the bill, Ed steered Annie, who was slightly tipsy from the wine, to their room. His eyes gleamed as he led her to the bed. He was humming a song.

"What is that, Ed? It sounds like that song, *Afternoon Delight*, that was a hit by the Starlight Vocal Band in the late 1970s." Annie laughed.

Ed smirked. "Yes, it is. I had other plans for us after our massages this afternoon, but as you know, I was so relaxed I sacked out. While it's not afternoon, the sentiment still stands." He began singing the lyrics, changing them to 'evening delight,' stretching out the letters in the word, 'evening.' Annie grinned but didn't object and responded in kind to Ed's passionate kisses. *Romantic interludes are not just for young people,* she thought to herself many minutes later. Then she fell peacefully asleep in Ed's arms.

Chapter 34

No leads. A cold case. Ed and Carrie could find no motive for George's murder, and no suspects. They were sitting in her office discussing the case a few days after he and Annie had returned from their trip to Canada.

"My friend from the CIA hasn't called me back. Maybe he couldn't get clearance to speak with me, although he's reliable, and I'm hoping he'll call me as a courtesy at some point. Still, I've pretty much written off that connection."

"I'm disappointed too, Ed. I still hope we'll learn something that will help us find George's murderer; we just have to be vigilant."

"Remember, Annie and I are leaving for our trip to England at the beginning of June and will be gone for ten days."

"If the murder isn't solved by the time you and Annie leave, Ed, I'm going to keep working on it while you're away. If I haven't arrested the killer by the time you get back, then you can resume the investigation. I don't want to close this case yet, and for now there's still money in the budget to pay you."

"Carrie, I'd do this one *pro bono*. I want to find George's killer as much as you do. Sally and her family need closure. We all do."

"Thanks, Ed."

Ed changed the subject. "Do you have plans for Saturday? Annie asked me to invite you, Matt and Natalya to our annual Memorial Day picnic. It will be a small group: our kids and grandkids; Amanda; Suzanne and Garrett; and our friends, the Beauvoirs. We invited Sally and her family, but they declined. They're not quite ready to socialize."

"I'll check with Matt about his work schedule; in any case, I'll bring Natalya."

"We plan to eat around 6:00, but I'm going to take the grandkids out on the pontoon around 2:30 for a couple hours. You and Natalya are welcome to join us."

"You have life vests for little ones?'

"Of course, we do. Remember, we have three grandchildren. We have one small enough for Natalya."

"I'd love to do that, Ed. Let's plan on it."

"I'll pack snacks and drinks for the kids, and then after we get back you're welcome to put Natalya down for a nap before dinner. We have a crib in one of our guest rooms."

"Sounds great. I look forward to it."

Ed cell phone rang as he was getting to his car. He didn't recognize the number and was tempted to let it go to voice mail. He answered anyway, hoping it might be Samir.

"Hello, this is Ed,"

"Hi, Ed, it's Samir. Sorry I didn't get back to you before now. I'm going to be in Ithaca at Cornell next Wednesday to give a lecture to a seminar of Ph.D. students in the graduate school of government. Any chance of meeting me for lunch that day? I have some information that I'd rather give to you in person."

"I have no other commitments that day. What time and where?"

"How about noon? I'll reserve a small meeting room in the building where I'm speaking, have sandwiches brought in." He gave Ed the address and room number at the university, and the two ended their conversation.

Ed was more than curious and couldn't wait to speak with his old friend.

Chapter 35

The forecast for Memorial Day weekend was perfect: low-to-mid 70s; gentle wind coming from the northwest, and clear skies. Ed helped Annie set up tables and chairs for the picnic, cleaned the grill and at a little past 2:30, gathered the grandchildren, Carrie and Natalya for the afternoon pontoon ride. Matt, as it turned out, was working that day; he would arrive in time for dinner.

The group assembled at 6:00 and was sitting out back enjoying drinks and appetizers while Ed grilled burgers and hot dogs. Annie had prepared Ellie's Beans, a crockpot recipe created by her dear friend, Ellen Connor, who had recently passed away after a long and heroic battle with cancer. Guests provided additional sides, beverages and desserts.

As they mingled and munched, they could hear the pleasant drone of motorboats on the lake, and from restaurants in the village, the sounds of rock bands playing on the decks. Just before dusk, they set up chairs facing west to watch a spectacular sunset over the lake, the fiery orange ball disappearing with a flash of green as it reached the horizon.

Annie and Ed fell into bed around midnight, exhausted. The next morning, the couple would be working as volunteers, helping to sign in participants for the triathlon that the Neighborhood Association organized. After that, Ed planned to write some notes in preparation for his meeting in Ithaca, and Annie vowed to start a list of clothing they would need for their trip to England.

Chapter 36

A few days later, Ed drove to Ithaca for his meeting with Samir. He gave himself a little extra time to stop at a winery on the western shore of Cayuga Lake to replenish the bottles of Dry Rosé and Riesling that had been favorites at the picnic. It was a cloudy and windy day, and the gray lake churned with angry looking white caps.

At just before noon, he entered the building at Cornell. A security guard directed him to the room where he was warmly greeted by his friend, Samir, a tall, slender man with short, dark curly hair and shining brown eyes. The two men hugged and then, after a few minutes of small talk, sat down across from each other at a long, rectangular table where a plate of sandwiches, chips, and pitchers of lemonade and water had been placed between them.

"Thanks for making the trip to Ithaca, Ed. What I'm going to tell you is strictly confidential; you can't even tell Annie or the police chief about our conversation."

"That's no problem. Annie has always understood, from the time I was working as a SEAL and now as a criminal consultant, that I'm not always at liberty to share sensitive information.

"Carrie and I have worked together before, and she won't press me when I tell her I can't share certain details from our meeting."

Motioning to the pitchers, Samir asked Ed what he'd like to drink. After indicating his preference for lemonade, the CIA officer filled two glasses and handed one to his friend.

He got straight to the point. "While I can assure you that George's murder had nothing to do with the CIA, Averill Wright heard correctly, Ed. There was a death threat against George years ago, but I couldn't talk with you about it over the phone."

Chapter 37

While George was a teaching fellow, Samir explained, he'd bonded with a student named Alex Pulcov. Alex was Russian on both sides of his family. His maternal grandparents had emigrated to New York City more than 40 years earlier with their two children, Alex's mother Olga, and his uncle, Dimitri. His paternal grandparents had emigrated several years before his father, Sergei, was born.

Many years later, Dimitri obtained a Ph.D. from Columbia and was hired as a professor of Russian Studies at the University of Pittsburgh and moved there with his wife, Dora, and their two small children. Dora, also a Russian immigrant, obtained a job at a settlement school, teaching English as a second language.

An only child, Alex was adopted by his uncle and aunt after his parents died in a car crash when he was nine. His uncle was genuinely fond of the boy. Dora, despite agreeing to the adoption, resented his intrusion into their lives and treated him unkindly.

Other than Dimitri, Dora and his cousins, Alex had no living relatives and when he was in his early teens, he became curious about his heritage. His uncle introduced him to Russian literature, history, art, politics and culture, and was teaching him the language.

After graduating from high school, Alex moved to Massachusetts to attend Boston College and declared dual majors in Russian Studies and business administration. During spring break in his junior year, something unsettling happened. He'd been visiting his family and one afternoon on a walk, Dimitri asked him questions that led the young man to suspect his uncle might be a Russian spy.

Alex feared that his curiosity about his heritage had led his uncle to believe that he'd developed an allegiance to his family's country of origin. Nothing could have been further from the truth. He was extremely patriotic and grateful that his grandparents' move to the United States had given him freedoms that he knew evaded ordinary Russian citizens.

His suspicions were correct. At first, Dimitri gently prodded him; the young man's answers to his questions were purposely vague. His uncle must have misunderstood his responses; before the break ended, he attempted to entice his nephew to work with him as an agent for the Russians.

Alex, appalled, had no intention of becoming a traitor to the U.S, and he was angry that his uncle had put him in such a difficult position. If he did nothing, he was betraying his own country. If he reported his uncle's deception, it would destroy his relationship with his family.

Trying to buy time, he promised he'd consider it. After much agonizing, he decided to speak confidentially to George, a man he admired and trusted. He was aware of George's military background and hoped his instructor might be able to guide him about the course of action he should take.

As it turned out, Alex's instincts were good. George had contacts at the CIA and after reporting Alex's conversation, was informed that Dimitri had been on their radar screen. They had recently verified he was a spy and planned to arrest him. They believed his wife may have known and approved of her husband's activities; however, they determined she was not working with him so would remain free but under surveillance.

Prior to his arrest, a mole within the Agency alerted Dimitri that his cover had been blown. He escaped to Miami where another Russian operative was waiting for him at a marina with a boat to take him to Cuba; from there, he'd fly to Moscow. The boat never arrived in Cuba. It exploded, killing all on board, conveniently in international waters.

"Was it an accident or were either we or the Russians responsible?"

Samir shook his head. "That's not our modus operandi. He would have ended up in one of our prisons or been traded for one of our operatives on *their* radar screen. For some reason, they'd discovered that he had tried recruiting his nephew, which, without getting clearance from his superiors was a huge mistake, one the Russians wouldn't take lightly. We expect they were also concerned about what he might reveal under questioning if he were caught before he reached Cuba. Dimitri had turned into a huge liability for them."

"Did you find the mole?" Ed asked.

"We did; it was one of our officers who'd been having an affair with Dimitri, unbeknownst to his wife. He had sought her out, and she thought he was a college professor, but at some point, after she fell madly in love with him, he confided to her that he was a spy. We believe Dimitri had intentionally seduced her to obtain information of a confidential nature that I can't discuss with you. She was apprehended and served many years in prison."

"What happened to Alex?" asked Ed.

"Dora suspected Alex had been instrumental in causing Dimitri's death and sent him a vicious and threatening letter. Her rage was out of control, and he feared for his life."

Chapter 38

"What a courageous young man," Ed remarked. "It must have been a gut-wrenching decision for him to speak with George, and I can only imagine how guilty he must have felt after learning his uncle had died."

"Yes, he loved his uncle and never imagined such a tragic outcome. Still, his conscience wouldn't allow him to ignore what he'd learned about him. He grieved, but with support from George, eventually made peace with his decision to report him.

"Dora's family had ties to the Russian mob, and the agency feared she would put a hit out on Alex. To protect him, we affected his death and set him up with a new identity. Dora was notified he'd died in a car accident in Boston.

"He decided, with our support and financial backing, to complete his bachelor's degree under his new name at Northwestern University in Illinois and changed his major to International Studies. Staying in Boston was too risky.

"We kept him on our radar screen. He was incredibly intelligent and had many attributes, including fluency in the Russian language and a proven ability to make difficult decisions. Shortly before he graduated, we contacted him and asked him to consider coming to work for us. He accepted, but before receiving his training, we required him to serve time in law enforcement or the military. To honor George, he joined the Navy and became a SEAL."

Ed had been listening to Samir's explanation with great interest, the wheels turning in his mind as the story evolved.

"You're positive the Russians weren't aware of George's involvement in outing Dimitri? Any chance they knew and bided their time and killed him?"

"Digitalis would never be their drug of choice, Ed. Their current method of assassination is to use newer, state-of-the-art nerve agents that make the victim suffer a horrible death. There was little possibility that George had been murdered by the Russians; still we decided to investigate, in case our assumption was incorrect. I can assure you they weren't responsible."

"What about the threatening letter?"

"Dora, Dimitri's wife, sent that one, too. Her husband was dead and so, she thought, was Alex. Her rage continued to grow. Alex had mentioned his friendship with George when he was home on one of his breaks. She surmised that he had been involved in outing Dimitri. He became the target of her vitriol.

"No return address or fingerprints were on the letter, and it was typed on a basic early model Underwood. But the postmark was from a post office in the same neighborhood where Dora lived. We discovered that Dora sent the letter to frighten George but didn't really plan to harm him."

Chapter 39

Ed had never expected his meeting with Samir would reveal a scenario appropriate for a cloak-and-dagger spy movie.

"How can you be sure?" Ed asked.

"If she had ordered a hit on George, it would have happened quickly and without warning. Shortly after she sent the letter, she emigrated to Russia with her two children. We let her go; we believed she had no knowledge of compromising state secrets. Despite his indiscretions, it's doubtful Dimitri kept her completely in the loop, even though she had pro-Russian political sentiments.

"Dora lived in Moscow for many years. She'd been employed in a low-level government position and died a few years ago of cancer. Her two grown children still live there and, as far as we know, are ordinary citizens with families of their own. They've never visited the United States since relocating, we're positive neither of them was involved in murdering George."

Ed didn't know what to say. Now he was even more frustrated since he was no closer to solving his friend's murder than he'd been weeks ago.

"Samir, I'm confused. Why go to this much trouble for a retired Navy SEAL turned financial adviser? It doesn't make sense to me." Then it hit him.

"George was an officer, wasn't he? And Peter Rigby, the man I interviewed at Barrow and Croft, he's Alex Pulcov, isn't he?"

Samir nodded and smiled. "I knew you'd figure it out."

"Monica Snyder said that she could vouch for not only all the employees at the firm but also the clients, and she's certain none of them could have murdered George. If that's the case, is the office a front for the CIA and are any of them really licensed financial advisors?"

"All the employees at Barrow and Croft are licensed and certified financial advisors, Ed; that's why we required George to get his master's degree in finance, and then his license and certification. But they're also vetted and trained CIA officers who work as a team to investigate money laundering and other crimes related to terrorism."

"Do any of them serve regular clients?"

Samir replied, "Of course. Even CIA employees need financial advisors they can trust to handle their investments."

"So, what you're saying is that all the clients also work for the CIA," Ed stated.

His friend shrugged his shoulders and smiled.

"The information you're giving me is way more than I expected, Samir, and I must admit I'm a bit stunned. But I also appreciate your trusting me and, as I promised, it won't go any farther."

Then another thought occurred to Ed. "Is there any possibility that Rigby sacrificed his uncle to show his loyalty to the Russians and is a double agent who's been working for them all along?"

"No, absolutely not. Peter was nowhere near Lighthouse Cove for days before and after George's murder, including the day of the memorial service. He was at a briefing in Europe. He truly regretted not being able to attend. The story of a family emergency was a cover. The circumstances that required him to be out of the country took precedence."

"You're absolutely certain about Rigby?"

Samir sighed. "Yes. George had been his mentor and confidant since Alex, now Peter, confided in him while he was studying in Boston. George was like a father to him and was the one who suggested we hire him to work at Barrow and Croft. They were not only a professional team, but also, as you know, close friends."

Chapter 40

Ed's head was spinning. He and Samir took a break to eat their lunch, and after, the conversation resumed. Samir explained that the CIA had recruited George before he left the Navy. He was interested but adamant that he be able to bring Sally into the loop. He'd be required to attend training sessions away from home in addition to getting the advanced degree in finance, and he said he wouldn't accept the position if he had to lie to her about the reason.

Samir said George was given clearance to confide in his wife. She was trustworthy, and while George was not an agent working outside the country as a spy, the work he did required discretion. The couple never informed Lily, George's parents, other family members or friends.

Ed said, "Samir, I don't understand why you felt the need to meet with me. All you had to tell me over the phone was that George's death had nothing to do with the CIA. That would have ended this line of inquiry, and it's all I needed to know."

Samir responded, "It's probably a matter of time before Sally remembers that George's life had been threatened many years ago in Boston. She knew about the letter, and he confided in her later that day that his father had overhead his conversation with one of his superiors about Dora's letter.

"We decided to be forthcoming because we didn't want you to be caught off guard if she says something about it; she's free to speak with you as the investigator into his murder. If the incident comes up in conversation, you can assure her you've spoken with us and there's no Russian connection to George's death. She'll be discreet and keep it to herself. Still, he was one of ours, and we'd appreciate your letting us know when you find his killer."

A short time later while driving home, Ed reflected on the meeting. He believed Samir, but now he was back to square one. He'd reassure Averill that there'd been no connection between George's death and anything having to do with the CIA but didn't like having to lie to the older man about his son's involvement with the Agency. He remembered Annie telling him that Sally said she and George kept no secrets from each other; he didn't realize at the time how true that was.

Deciding he'd wait until tomorrow to ponder next steps, Ed turned on the radio to a classical jazz station and tried to relax. He was looking forward to having his nightly cocktail with Annie. He could summarize the results of his meeting with Samir, but he was frustrated that he couldn't divulge any of the details. He knew she wouldn't push him for answers, but he trusted her more than anyone and would dearly have loved to confide in her.

Chapter 41

The next morning, Ed called Carrie, briefed her about his meeting with Samir and that George's death had nothing to with the CIA or a Russian connection.

"I'm not surprised, Ed. We both knew it was a long shot. Since that one's off the table, what's your plan now?"

"I don't know, Carrie. I'm running out of ideas."

"Let's meet this morning in my office. I have some thoughts that might put us back on track."

"I can be there in less than ten minutes."

"I'll see you soon."

A short while later, Ed was sitting in front of Carrie's desk while she fiddled with her laptop. She turned it towards him and opened a screen. On it was a photo of a small, white pill.

"What is this?" she asked.

"A little white pill," he responded.

Carrie minimized the screen and opened another. "And this?"

"An identical little white pill."

"Aha! That's what most people would think. In fact, these two pills are not identical. Look closely, they have different numbered codes." She enlarged the photos.

"You could've fooled me. What's your point?"

The police chief explained. "One pill is aspirin; the other digitalis."

"And??" Ed asked.

"Instead of being murdered, maybe George was accidentally poisoned by someone who happened to be hiking through the cemetery while he was working there. The two started talking, and perhaps during the conversation, George mentioned he'd developed a headache. I researched beta blockers; a headache can be a side effect. The hiker, who carried both drugs with him, believed he was offering George an aspirin but instead accidentally gave him digitalis."

Ed hesitated for a few seconds before responding, "That's a bit of a stretch, don't you think? The two meds would have been in easily identifiable bottles; it's hard to imagine someone mixing them up."

"Not necessarily." Carrie typed something on her keyboard. A small, clear, oval-shaped plastic container, hinged in the middle, appeared on the screen.

"This is a pill container, Ed. Sometimes people carry these with them instead of bottles when they need to take medicine during the day. See, there's an AM on one side and a PM on the other. It's possible one of the meds was in the AM side; the other on the PM, and the hiker got confused or wasn't paying attention and gave George the wrong drug."

"You're assuming this hiker has a heart condition and carried both medicines with him?"

"Yes. Aspirin is supposed to help if someone is experiencing heart attack symptoms, and this person might have had to take the digitalis at prescribed intervals."

"If it was an accidental poisoning why didn't he call 911 after George started exhibiting symptoms?"

"If you remember, digitalis isn't particularly fast acting, he may have walked away before the drug took effect and not have realized what he'd done."

Ed, skeptical, responded, "Annie believes George found something of value at the cemetery that morning.

Couldn't it also be possible that he showed it to someone with a heart condition who recognized its value? When George wasn't looking, he slipped the drug into the to-go cup, certain it would kill him and waited until he was dead to steal it?"

"I suppose, but my interpretation could also be accurate. Please give me a little credit for thinking outside the box here, Ed."

"Neither of us knows for sure what happened that morning, Carrie. Since we're not making headway with our current line of inquiry, I'm going to start investigating whether George was murdered for something he found."

Carrie, testy, replied, "Go ahead, but at the same time, I plan to look into whether his death might have been the result of accidental poisoning. I'm going to schedule a press conference indicating that we believe someone may have visited the cemetery that day who knows what happened to George. If his death was accidental, we're not looking to prosecute; we just want to know the truth."

"We're both frustrated, Carrie. I guess it can't hurt to explore both angles," Ed acknowledged. "We certainly have nothing else to go on."

PART TWO
Chapter 42

Ed called Carrie several days later. No one had come forward after the press conference to admit they'd been at the cemetery the day George died and had accidentally given him the wrong medicine. Discouraged, she acknowledged that perhaps Annie was correct in believing the murderer had killed George for something he found at the cemetery. Ed gave her credit for trying and said he hoped there would be a break in the case while he and Annie were in England.

After an easy flight into Heathrow, a hotel shuttle took Ed and Annie to their hotel in London—The Drury Lane Inn. Situated in Covent Gardens, it was located within a short walk to Piccadilly Circus, the Theatre District and a multitude of excellent pubs and restaurants. Annie's friend, Donna Jones, had recommended the property, promising they would adore the cozy atmosphere and warm hospitality.

A comfortable lobby with a warming fireplace was the site for evening cocktails for guests, and an onsite restaurant served simple, delicious English fare. Annie adored the full English breakfasts and gorged herself on buttery English cheeses, crisply toasted crumpets, an array of delectable preserves, smoky kippers and mugs of English Breakfast tea. Ed dug into eggs made to order, savory and sweet scones, mouth-watering rashers of bacon and rich, hot coffee.

"I'm not going to fit into my clothes if I keep eating like this," Annie groaned the first morning after finishing her second crumpet and adding generous amounts of rich, whole milk and delicious, locally produced wildflower honey to her tea.

"You'll work it off," Ed grinned. And then leered.

"Ed!" Annie laughed.

"What I meant is that we're going to walk a lot during this trip, Annie," he replied innocently, his eyes sparkling with humor.

Annie swatted at him, "You're like a randy teenager." With a Cheshire cat grin, she said, "please don't stop. I love it."

Later that morning, they hailed a taxi and went to Buckingham Palace to view the changing of the guard, then stopped for lunch at a charming pub where they each ordered a Ploughman's lunch: crusty bread with butter; more of the wonderful English cheese; an assortment of pickles; and warm English ale.

Their first stop after lunch was a visit to the Millennial Ferris Wheel where, soaring above the city, they marveled at London's skyline. They spent the rest of afternoon exploring the Tower of London and Westminster Abbey. Annie, who in college had majored in social work and minored in English, got chills as she stood over Shakespeare's grave and the graves of William Blake, Jane Austen and Noel Coward.

They returned to the hotel in time for drinks and dinner. Exhausted, they fell asleep early, excited about their visit the next day to the Victoria and Albert Museum.

Chapter 43

Donna Jones greeted the DeCleryks at the entrance of the museum. "Let's go to the King's Treasures' exhibit first since that's what you came to see," she suggested. "All the pieces have been cleaned, polished and restored; it's a gorgeous collection."

She led the pair through a long, wide corridor at the end of which was a broad niche with a table and upon it an enclosed glass case that displayed a jewel-encrusted brooch, earrings, scabbard and snuff box, remarkably intact. The exhibit was illuminated with recessed ceiling lights. Annie gasped.

"They're beautiful, Donna. They were so dirty and dull after Ed found them; I never expected they would look like this."

"The royal family will be forever grateful that you discovered them, Ed, and for making sure they were returned to us."

After a few minutes, as Ed and Annie quietly viewed the sparkling precious jewelry-encrusted artifacts, Donna announced, "I have something else I want to show you."

"Are you going to tell us about it or keep us in suspense?" Annie asked.

Donna smiled. "After his death, the heirs of the recently deceased Baron Robert William Fitzhugh donated a huge collection of cloisonné to this museum, dating back to the early 1800s."

Annie's eyes lit up. "Fitzhugh, as in Robert Fitzhugh who was one of Lighthouse Cove's heroes of the War of 1812?"

"Yes; interesting that there's yet another connection between Lighthouse Cove and England, don't you think? Come with me."

The pair followed Donna through the museum to an archway that led into a small room with tall glass cases. Security cameras on the ceiling and a blinking alarm system had been put in place to deter anyone who might attempt to get into the cases to touch or steal the artifacts.

Ed looked at the collection and whispered, "Oh my," while Annie just shook her head. Lining the shelves were hundreds of enamel and jewel-encrusted time pieces, vases, brooches, bowls, urns, ornaments and small keepsake boxes.

"It appears that Robert Fitzhugh's father, William, was so enamored with the intricacies of the technique that bonded jewels or stones to metal that he started collecting items at the beginning of the 19th century.

"The family continued the tradition until recently. The current Baron Fitzhugh, Edward Percival, and his wife, Miranda, decided to downsize and move into their townhouse in London after his father died. They deeded the estate to the Preservation Society; the mansion and gardens will be maintained and open to the public. They donated the entire collection to this museum. Pretty incredible, eh?"

"It's actually a bit overwhelming," Annie responded. "Did you meet the family when they donated the pieces?"

"No, I would have liked to, but they worked with our director who provided me with all the details about the collection, and I curated it. I read Amanda Fitzhugh's book about her ancestor when I ran the museum in Lighthouse Cove, so it's especially meaningful to me."

"It must be worth millions," Annie remarked.

"It is. And what's even more remarkable is that each successive generation of Fitzhugh collectors kept a log of what was acquired, the purchase price and a description. Only one piece is missing."

"What is it?" Ed asked.

"It's a pocket watch that William Fitzhugh gave to his son, Robert, before he left for the states. When Robert returned to England, it wasn't in his possession. It had his initials engraved on the back and a small latch that opened to reveal a space for something personal to be inserted, like a lock of hair or small note.

"No one in the family has information about what happened to the watch; it's assumed that Robert lost it during the skirmish in Lighthouse Cove or that his wife, Rebecca, had hidden it for safekeeping. As you know, she and her daughters emigrated to England after her husband was captured and tried for treason and never returned to the U.S. The watch was never recovered."

Like a wisp of smoke, a thought came into Ed's mind but dissipated before he could capture it. He was certain it had something to do with George's murder, but he had vowed not to think about the case on this trip so put it aside.

"I can't wait to tell Amanda about this, Donna," Annie exclaimed. "As you know from reading her book, Fitzhugh was her ancestor. She's never mentioned anything about this collection and probably has no idea these items are part of her family history. I wish she could see this. She's in her 80s and having some physical issues, so I don't expect a trip to England is in her future."

"For security purposes we're not supposed to let visitors take photos, but I can look the other way while you take a few for her."

Chapter 44

George Wright's killer slept soundly for the first time in weeks. The coast was clear. Ed DeCleryk and his meddlesome wife, Annie, had left the country. That young female police chief hadn't a clue about how to investigate a murder, and the old woman...well, that issue would be resolved. Soon. Very soon. The killer chuckled.

No suspects had surfaced, how frustrating for the investigators, and the killer believed that for the present and the near future, they would keep on running into dead ends. Haha. Dead ends. That awful man's life had ended with him dead at the end of a path in a cemetery. Fitting end. Dead end. Pretty amusing. The investigators had no knowledge that another death had occurred, earlier, much earlier, many years ago, that had also never been discovered. Luck, always luck, the killer thought.

There had been no clear intention to kill George Wright, at least not at first. Then the killer feared he might have guessed, might have figured it out; something had to be done. And quickly. People would say, "Poor George." In the killer's estimation, not really. They'd say, "Poor family." Hardly. They'd get over it. One always did.

The killer knew about loss, so despite some misgivings, figured that George deserved what he got. Now no one would ever know about the deception. No one could ever possibly figure out that George's death was a protective act. One that would shield many from the full and disturbing truth. They'd believe what they would, and that was a good thing. With some regret the killer acknowledged one more must die, to protect and preserve. That's the way it would be for now and forever.

156 Murder in the Cemetery

Chapter 45

Jason was making progress on the War of 1812 brochure. He had a few more questions for Amanda and decided to call her one morning to schedule another interview. He'd become fond of the warm and gracious elderly woman and looked forward to spending time with her, perhaps she'd invite him to stay for a cup of tea and freshly baked scones.

She'd admitted to him during one of their meetings that despite wanting a family, she and her late husband had never been able to have children. His own grandparents were long gone, and he hoped he might become, for her, a surrogate grandchild.

He picked up the phone and dialed her number, and she answered on the third ring, delighted he had called. He asked to visit with her that day. She responded that she was working at her church's rummage sale until noon and then afterward she and her close friend, Eleanor Brown, were going to Birdie's Tearoom for a light luncheon. She suggested he meet her at her house between 1:30 and 2:00; she might want to pick up a few groceries at the market after lunch. She volunteered that while she didn't have scones, she'd baked oatmeal raisin cookies the previous evening.

Jason rang Amanda's doorbell at 1:45. She didn't answer. He noticed the door was slightly ajar and wondered if she had forgotten to latch it when she left that morning or after she returned home and hadn't heard the bell ring. He rang the bell again, and this time after hearing no response and hoping he was doing the right thing, he opened the door.

He called out, "Mrs. Reynolds, it's me, Jason Shipley." Again, no answer. He thought perhaps she was running late, then became alarmed when he saw that all the drawers in an antique chest in the foyer had been opened, their contents strewn on the floor. Even more concerned, he called out again. "Mrs. Reynolds, are you here?"

He cautiously approached the living room, and his breath caught. A secretary had been ransacked; papers, pencils and office supplies scattered about. Then he saw her. She was lying on the floor, face-down, right hand stretched out holding her cell phone. He knelt next to her and put his hand on her neck. She had a pulse, but it was slow; she was breathing, but barely.

Terrified and shaking, he got out his cell phone and called 911. "Hello. My name is Jason Shipley. I'm at the home of Amanda Reynolds on Bay Street. I want to report a burglary, and it appears she's been attacked. She's unconscious."

The dispatcher asked, "What's the street number?"

"2901, please get here ASAP," he pleaded.

Sitting on the floor next to his friend, the young man felt a strong breeze coming from the back of the house. He got up, ran into the kitchen and noticed that the back door was wide open. He believed Amanda must have returned home from her outing to interrupt a burglary, and eager to escape, the burglars may have pushed the elderly lady, knocking her out, then exited through that door.

Seconds later, he heard sirens and breathed a sigh of relief. After a sharp rap on the door, Carrie and Mia along with two EMTs entered the house. The EMTs quickly administered CPR, inserted an IV and moved and strapped Amanda to a gurney.

"She's still alive, son." The EMT commended Jason. "Calling us may have saved her. Good work." They left quickly, and, sirens blaring, took off for Newark Hospital.

Trembling with anxiety and fear, Jason gave his statement to Carrie, then after he was permitted to leave, Mia affixed a yellow crime scene tape on the door. Later that afternoon, the pair would examine the home for prints and other evidence that would hopefully shed light on who had committed the crime.

After getting into his car, on impulse Jason decided to drive to the hospital. The poor woman had no family and at least he could provide her with emotional support. He hoped she'd recover.

He parked in the parking lot and headed for the emergency room. Amanda had been moved to a curtained cubicle, and medical personnel were working on her as he arrived. He checked at the desk. The receptionist wouldn't tell him anything; he was not family.

"I don't think she has any living relatives." He introduced himself. "I'm a friend. Can't you at least tell me what her condition is?"

A resident who had been completing paperwork at the desk heard the interaction and responded, "She's just following protocol. Let me see what I can find out."

After a few minutes he returned, looking somber. Jason dreaded what was coming.

"She's alive. She may have been physically assaulted; the attending doctor found bruises on her body, but they also may be the result of the fall."

He shook his head and continued, "It does appear she may have had a heart incident or TIA, possibly brought on from fright; the doctor said he'll do some testing but won't have the results back for several hours."

Jason, upset, asked if Amanda was going to die.

"I'm sorry, I can't tell you that. It's not necessary that you stay, there's nothing you can do for her, but why don't you give me your phone number? I promise I'll call you later with an update on her condition."

Reluctant to leave, Jason gave the resident his number. He considered calling Annie in England but decided against it. She couldn't do anything, and it didn't make sense to interrupt her trip and upset her. Suzanne Gordon had rescheduled classes that day to work at the museum in Annie's absence; he'd go back there and report to her what had happened to Amanda.

A few minutes after he left the hospital, Dr. Maria Cisneros, while making her rounds, was walking through the emergency room and noticed Amanda on a bed in a cubicle. The physician in attendance was Carrie Ramos' husband, Matt. She walked over to him and reading his nametag, introduced herself to the handsome, dark-haired man.

"Dr. Ramos, I'm Maria Cisneros. I don't think we've met before. I'm an internist in Wolcott and am here doing rounds. Amanda Reynolds is one of my patients. What's wrong with her?"

Matt responded, "It appears her home was burgled this afternoon, and she must have interrupted it and been attacked. We won't know exactly what's wrong until we get results from the tests. Has she had heart or circulatory issues recently?"

Maria shook her head. "No. Other than bone and joint issues that come with being in her 80s, she's in great health. Her blood pressure is normally low, and her EKGs have been perfect.

"She takes no medicines. I've prescribed some for her arthritis, but she says between exercise and herbal remedies, she doesn't need them. She's due for her six-month checkup, and I suppose her medical situation could have changed over these past months, but in that case, she would have called and made an earlier appointment. She's responsible."

Maria asked Matt to call her with the test results and suggested they do a consultation about next steps after that. A room had become available in the cardiac ward; for now, until they determined the diagnosis, they would move her to that floor.

Chapter 46

Dr. Cisneros completed her rounds and went back to her office. She had finished seeing her last patient of the day and had started reviewing Amanda Reynolds' file when the phone rang. She glanced at the clock; it was just after 4:30.

"Hi, Maria. It's Matt Ramos. I have the results from Amanda Reynolds' tests. You're sure she didn't have a heart condition?"

"Positive, Matt. I was just reading her file. Why do you ask?"

"We may have a problem. She had a small dose of digitalis in her system. Not enough to kill her, just enough to cause her heart to slow down and precipitate a collapse. My wife, Carrie, is the police chief of Lighthouse Cove, and she's been keeping me informed of the investigation into George Wright's death. I know that drug killed him and called her a few minutes ago. I'm wondering if whoever killed George may have also attempted to kill Amanda."

After thanking Matt for the update, Maria hung up the phone with a terrible sinking feeling. *Oh, no,* she thought. *Amanda is a patient here, and so was George. Perhaps Mary Williams isn't innocent after all. Maybe our giving her a second chance wasn't the right thing to do. Maybe she's responsible for both poisonings, but why?*

She rang Irwin Shaw's intercom and asked that he come to her office immediately. He arrived within seconds. She summarized her conversation with Matt

Ramos. "I think we need to check the drug supply closet, Irwin; hopefully no more bottles of digitalis are missing. "

"I'll be right back," he responded.

He returned after about ten minutes. "All bottles of digitalis are there, and Mary has never examined Amanda; in fact, Mary wasn't even working the day Amanda had her last appointment. I'm certain she's not involved with this."

Maria Cisneros replied, "I'm so relieved, but now I'm feeling guilty that I even thought about her as a suspect. I guess it's going to take me a while to fully trust her, despite knowing in my heart that I made the right decision to hire her full time."

She continued, "I'm delighted that Amanda is going to be okay, but I'm thinking that there must be a connection between what happened to her and George's death. Mary's in the clear, but if not her, then who could possibly want them dead?"

From the letters of Rebecca Fitzhugh

July,1816
My dear Marigold,
We arrived at the Port of London a fortnight ago, and I had intended to write long before now. We've been caught up in a whirlwind of activity from the time we disembarked.

Robert's parents have been lovely and gracious. They live on an estate north of London, with acres and acres of land, a large manor house, and stables. A gamekeeper lives with his family in a cottage on the premises. Thankfully, they keep no slaves, but there are many servants who are treated respectfully and provided with spacious and clean quarters.

Patience and Charity love their newly met grandparents who seem to dote on them. I have cautioned my in-laws, however, that my girls should not be spoiled, and I don't want them to take for granted their new, privileged life. Nicely has settled in and is accepted as a family pet, which is a positive development, as the barn cats want nothing to do with her.

Oh, and the best news yet! Robert is with us. He has been pardoned, as I had hoped and prayed, and seems no worse for his experience, although he has lost some of his humor and is a bit dour. I never anticipated this outcome and praise God daily for giving my husband back to me.

To my dismay, my husband has decided we will not return to New York, though he is grateful for the time he lived in our country. His father is aging, and as the heir to the estate, he believes we must remain here. I am saddened by this turn of events but, to keep our family together, I will abide by his decision. I will never, however, be fully comfortable as a member of the aristocracy, and hope that before long, the children and I shall be able to return to New York for a lengthy visit with you and Remington.

I will write again, my dear sister. Please keep our family in your prayers.

With love,
Rebecca

Chapter 47

Carrie sat, head in hands, behind her desk. She and
Mia had just returned from Amanda's house. Matt had
called and reported she'd been poisoned with digitalis;
in addition to burglary and assault, whoever committed
the crime would also be charged with attempted
murder. She was certain it was the same person who
had killed George Wright.

After scouring the premises for fingerprints or other
evidence that could lead them to a suspect, they'd come
up empty-handed. Carrie felt overwhelmed, exhausted
and discouraged. For a split second, she regretted her
decision to become police chief. She had never
imagined that she'd be investigating two murders plus
an attempt on another's life in less than two years.

She questioned her ability to do the job successfully
and needed to talk to someone with experience about
how to proceed. She'd adored her former boss, Ben
Fisher, and picking up the phone dialed his number.
She felt way over her head and was confident he could
provide perspective.

Carrie felt much better after speaking with him.
"Look for the simplest explanation rather than trying to
make the investigation more complex than it should
be," he advised. "But be sure to continue to think
outside the box. You and Ed will solve this case
eventually, be patient."

She picked up a piece of chalk and walked over to
the blackboard that was affixed to one wall in her office
and started writing. What did George and Amanda have

in common? It had been determined they hadn't known one another, but they both used the same medical practice. Mary Williams had been ruled out as a suspect, and it seemed that no one else at the practice had a motive.

Could anything else link Amanda's attack and George's murder? She thought for a moment. Amanda Reynolds was an expert on the War of 1812, and Ed and Annie believed George's death was the result of something he'd discovered at the cemetery where casualties of that war were buried. The person who killed George must believe that Amanda possessed something related to his discovery. Who? And what?

She recounted the sequence of events the day George died. It appeared he had walked to the cemetery and then home to get his truck and tools to begin the clean-up. He'd been found with a partially drunk cup of tea laced with a drug that, combined with one he was taking had killed him, plus a pastry he hadn't brought from home. The cup didn't have the Bistro Louise logo on it, Mike Garfield was convinced he must have stopped elsewhere.

But where? Then it hit her. It must have been The Cove; it had opened for the season the day George died. While patrons could eat in the small dining room, it was normally only open during inclement weather. On warm, sunny days, and the day George died was warm and sunny, patrons ate outside at picnic tables. Perhaps after purchasing his food, he'd invited someone he knew, or even a stranger, to sit with him.

The likelihood was that, for whatever reason, this person was in possession of digitalis and upon learning what George had discovered at the cemetery had deliberately poisoned him to steal it. The murderer may have known about George's medical condition or if not, realized that an overdose of the drug could kill someone or at the very least, render them unconscious.

She circled back to Jason Shipley; he appeared to be the common thread. He'd visited the cemetery the day George died, Amanda that same morning and was at her house again today claiming to have interrupted an attempted burglary. But was that what really happened? Or had he broken into her house while she was away and accosted and poisoned her upon her return?

Carrie called the museum, hoping to speak with him. Suzanne answered. In Annie's absence she had rescheduled some of her classes to work there for a few hours each day.

Jason had an alibi. Suzanne said he had spent the entire morning in his office, worked in the gift shop over lunch while the Kellys took a break, and left just minutes before his meeting with Amanda. She'd expected him back within the hour; then when he didn't return, she assumed he'd stayed longer for tea. He had called her on his way to the hospital to tell her what happened. "He's become quite fond of Amanda and is not only upset but also very frightened for her. I told him that after he left the hospital to go home."

She continued, "I've been wondering about something, Carrie. Could the link between Amanda's attack and George's murder be connected to the War of 1812?"

Carrie sighed. "Yes, I've come to the same conclusion. I just have no idea what that could be. I'm hoping to get some answers from Amanda as soon as she's able to talk, although she may be as much in the dark about what happened as we are."

Chapter 48

After getting clearance from her husband and Maria Cisneros to interview Amanda, Carrie left her office at 10 o'clock the next morning and headed for the hospital. Amanda was sitting up in bed drinking a cup of tea. Two security guards, per Carrie's recommendation and the hospital administrator's concurrence, sat outside her room. Carrie didn't want the killer to try and finish the job, now that the word was out that Amanda had survived the attack. She just wasn't sure how she was going to protect her once she came home.

"Mrs. Reynolds, I'm Carrie Ramos, the Lighthouse Cove police chief. Do you remember me? We've met before."

"Yes, of course I do, my dear; how lovely to see you. Would you like a cup of tea? I expect I can ring the nurses' station to have one brought to you."

"No, thanks. Are you able to answer some questions that might help us identify your attacker? We believe that person may also have killed George Wright. You were both poisoned with the same drug."

"Oh, my, that's dreadful," Amanda responded, her pale face becoming even paler. She volunteered that she remembered awakening yesterday at her usual time and after breakfasting and dressing, had walked across the street to her church, feeling strong enough to use her cane instead of her walker. She spent most of the morning helping with the rummage sale, then she and her friend, Eleanor, had gone to Birdie's Tearoom for a light lunch.

"It appears someone may have entered your house while you were away. Did you return home earlier than expected?"

Amanda looked flustered. "Yes, Eleanor and I had planned to go to the market after lunch, but I had a meeting with that sweet boy, Jason, and it was getting late, so instead, Eleanor drove me home. I expected to arrive between 1:30 and 2:00. I think it probably was a little earlier, around 1:15. I opened my door and had an eerie feeling, perhaps a premonition. Nothing seemed amiss though, until I noticed the chest in the foyer had been ransacked. I walked into the living room and took my cell phone out of my purse to call 911 and was grabbed from behind. I'm certain it was a man; he had large hands and was wearing gloves. In a gruff, muffled voice he murmured, 'You know what I want, where is it?' I replied I had no idea what he was talking about. That's the last I remember until I came to in this hospital."

"You were lucky, Amanda, that Jason had scheduled a meeting with you yesterday afternoon. He must have startled the intruder who escaped through the back door. Jason found you on the floor and called 911. His quick reaction probably saved your life."

"He's a lovely young man, and I'm grateful he found me. He sent flowers." She pointed to a vase with assorted spring flowers on a table, "and is planning to visit me later today."

"Have you received any unusual phone calls lately or seen anyone lurking outside your house?"

"I have received a couple of calls on my land line; they were hang-ups. Do you think someone was calling to determine if I were home?"

"That's possible. How would this person have gotten in? No locks were picked; the back door was wide open."

Amanda looked embarrassed. "I must confess. I never lock my doors; no one does in the village."

Carrie shook her head. Once Amanda was stabilized, she'd be released. The police chief feared she'd be vulnerable to another burglary and attack, and she simply didn't have staff to assign security detail to the woman. Still, she had to do something to keep her safe.

"Would you consider installing a security system in your house? I can get a reputable company to do that for you, but afterwards you'll have to keep your doors locked at all times."

Amanda at first resisted, insisting that she believed the attacker wouldn't try again. Carrie was emphatic; she relented.

"Do you have any relatives you could go and stay with for a while, at least until we get the system installed or arrest the person who did this to you?" Carrie asked.

Amanda shook her head. "Unfortunately, I have no living relatives, dear, in New York state that I'm aware of. Members of the Fitzhugh family, which was my maiden name, reside mainly in England, although there is supposedly a branch of the family that emigrated to the U.S. long after Robert Fitzhugh's death. I believe they may live in the mid-west, but I've not had contact with any of them. I won't impose on my friends. That could put them in harm's way."

"Because it's crucial to your safety and well-being, I think I can get the company to do a rush job and install the security system before you return home. In addition, I'll have Mia, our new policewoman, keep a closer eye on your house when she patrols the village. And I'll give you my cell phone number. You're to call me any time day or night if you feel threatened. Please promise me you'll do that." Amanda nodded.

"Upon your release from here, Mia will transport you home. Perhaps members of your church will help you put things away, but your house is still a crime scene, so before you do, you'll need to determine if anything was taken. If so, we'll amend our report."

Carrie left the hospital room, walked to the nurses' station, showed her badge and asked to have her husband, Matt, paged. She had a question for him.

Matt was just finishing up with a patient and met Carrie a few minutes later in the cafeteria. He smiled and gave her a quick kiss on the lips.

"It's not every day I get to see my beautiful wife during working hours. To what do I owe this pleasure, my beloved?" he asked with a smile and a gleam in his soulful dark eyes.

Rolling her eyes, Carrie smiled. "Oh, cut the blarney, Matt. You know this isn't a social call. I have questions about Amanda Reynolds' medical condition if you feel you can answer them without violating patient privacy laws."

He grinned. "Give me a minute. I'll go and ask Amanda, and if she consents to my speaking with you, HIPAA laws won't be violated."

He excused himself and returned ten minutes later, telling Carrie that Amanda had no problems with his discussing her medical condition as related to her attack and had signed a release form.

Carrie told Matt that Amanda's memory was sketchy; she had recalled being accosted and they knew she'd been poisoned, but had she been physically or sexually assaulted?

Matt responded that no bruises on her head or body were the result of being hit or punched; he assumed they were the result of her falling; fortunately, she'd not been sexually assaulted.

Carrie sighed. No fingerprints had been found in her house that weren't accounted for, and she'd been with people she knew and trusted before the incident happened. She was positive George's murder and Amanda's attack were connected; she just couldn't put the pieces together. Despite Ben's encouragement and optimism, the case had become more complex and no closer to being solved now than it had been weeks ago.

Chapter 49

Ed and Annie were sad their trip to England was coming to an end. They'd had a wonderful time and after viewing the exhibits at the museum had enjoyed side trips to Bath, Oxford, Cambridge, Stratford-upon-Avon, Warwick Castle and Stonehenge.

The weekend before they returned home, they traveled to Paris with Donna and her husband where they sampled light-as-air pastel-colored macarons and drank café au lait at a charming patisserie, admired the impressive artwork at the Louvre and took a multitude of photos of the Eiffel Tower and Arc de Triomphe.

One evening, after a leisurely stroll along the Seine, the two couples took a taxi to the West Bank where they feasted on simple bistro fare and drank carafes of inexpensive, delicious red wine at a charming sidewalk cafe. Feeling like honeymooners, Ed and Annie were grateful they'd been able to get away from Lighthouse Cove and the specter of George Wright's death hanging over them.

They hadn't heard from Carrie, and the only emails and calls they'd received were from their children and grandchildren who were curious about how they were enjoying their trip. As they were to discover, Carrie had purposely withheld information about the attack on Amanda, not wanting to upset them with the disturbing turn of events.

A day after they returned to Lighthouse Cove, Ed met with the police chief who apprised him of the latest development, noting that no additional leads had surfaced and despite exploring many different options including a link to the War of 1812, it appeared that the case had gone cold.

That night, over a simple dinner of roasted lemon chicken and a green bean and potato salad, Annie reminded Ed that the same thing had happened when he'd investigated Emily Bradford's murder. In the end, it had all worked out.

She took Ed's hand. "Please be patient, my dear. I have faith that you and Carrie will eventually figure out who is behind these horrible crimes and bring that person to justice. For some reason I have a feeling it may happen soon."

Chapter 50

We're not making progress with this investigation; something's missing, Ed thought early the next morning while sitting in his study drinking coffee. Then he had an idea.

He walked into the kitchen where Annie was baking cookies in anticipation of their grandchildren spending the weekend.

"Annie, I'm really frustrated that we haven't been able to make any headway in finding the person who killed George and attacked Amanda. We're all now on the same page that the crimes are related to the War of 1812, but we've run out of leads. I'm going to call and ask Carrie to meet with me here this afternoon to do some brainstorming She'll be less distracted than if we meet at her office. If you can spare the time, I'd appreciate your participating."

"I can do that, Ed, but after I finish baking, I need to go to work. As you know, this is the beginning of the busy season for me. I'll plan to be home by 4:00, we can start the meeting a few minutes later. We'll have to keep it short. I imagine Carrie will want to get home in time for dinner."

"I'll call her right now," Ed replied.

At 4:00, Ed, Annie and Carrie assembled around a small table in Ed's study. He'd affixed a white board on an easel and commenced, "There are crimes of passion, premeditated crimes, hate crimes, crimes of opportunity and familial crimes. We can rule out a hate crime and a crime of passion. George's murder was most likely not premeditated, and while it appears the burglary at Amanda's and her subsequent attack were, I'm positive the same person committed both crimes. What about opportunity or familial? Let's throw ideas out, whatever comes to mind, don't filter anything."

"What about a familial crime of opportunity, Ed?" Annie asked.

"What are you thinking, Annie?"

Annie looked at Carrie. "You checked the calls George made on his phone the day he died. Did he call anyone besides me?"

"Yes, he called his son-in-law, Eric. As you know, he's a professor at the University of Rochester, but he didn't have classes that day and was working from home. We talked at the luncheon after the funeral and he volunteered that George had suggested he bring the children to Lighthouse Cove for an early family dinner at The Brewery that evening, after Sally and Lily returned from Skaneateles. He declined. It was a busy day, and he said it wasn't going to work out."

"Did you believe him?" Annie queried.

"I had no reason not to. When I interviewed her, Sally reported that spontaneous meals together were pretty common in their family."

"Maybe that's not what happened," Annie remarked.

"What are you getting at, Annie? Do you believe Eric lied about the conversation?" Ed asked.

"Possibly. Eric teaches 19th century American history. Could his area of expertise be the War of 1812 and…."

Carrie interrupted, "and the real story is that after not being able to reach you on the phone, George called Eric and asked him to meet him at the cemetery which is where his son-in-law killed him after coveting whatever it was that George found."

"That's just what I was thinking, Carrie, and maybe those other set of tire tracks that we couldn't identify were his."

"We've met Eric, Annie. Does he strike you as a killer? He's bright, attractive and personable," Ed responded.

Annie rolled her eyes. "So was Ted Bundy, Ed."

"Bundy didn't have a relationship with family, Annie. The circumstances were quite different," Ed snapped back.

"I'm not suggesting Eric's a serial killer, Ed, just trying to make a point."

Carrie agreed with Annie. "Ed, maybe Eric's not another Ted Bundy, but you of all people know that looks and personality can be deceiving. Think about our last murder case. Eric could be a narcissistic sociopath who until now has kept his tendencies well-hidden. Killing his father-in-law wouldn't have bothered him if it was a means to an end to enhance his reputation in academic circles.

"He could have stolen and hidden the piece and months later purportedly discovered it while hiking in the woods. There must be lots of unrecovered artifacts from the period of history buried between here and Sackets Harbor."

"You both may have a point. But George died from a lethal combination of two drugs, and it would certainly be a stretch of the imagination to believe that Eric has a heart condition. Wouldn't Sally have mentioned that to you, Annie?"

Annie reflected. "Yes, but I just remembered something."

She proceeded to tell them that shortly after George was diagnosed with AFib, she'd had lunch with Sally. Her friend had mentioned that Eric's mother, Susan, had also been having health problems and was undergoing testing to determine what was wrong. Sally had been upset; the two women were close friends.

"Maybe she's the one with a heart condition," Annie remarked.

"Annie, you don't really know if that's true, or if it is, that the doctor prescribed digitalis and Eric had access to it. If he met George at the cemetery that day, the murder wouldn't have been premeditated so why would he be carrying the drug with him?" Ed argued.

Annie shrugged. "A crime of opportunity? It's possible that since Eric was working at home that day, his mother asked him to pick up a prescription for her and bring it to her later. He may have stopped on his way to Lighthouse Cove to get it, just like Jason did for his father.

"After recognizing the value of what George found, he managed to go back to his vehicle and get a pill or two that he slipped into his father-in-law's drink. Remember, that to-go cup had traces of the drug in the tea."

Carrie looked at Ed. "While you were away, Ed, I did some of my own brainstorming. Another possibility is that George called Eric and instead of asking him to meet him at the cemetery, requested they meet at The Cove. At first, I thought maybe it was Jason, but I ruled him out. So, it must be Eric. We know George didn't purchase his food at Bistro Louise, The Cove was the only other restaurant open for breakfast that day.

"After the two men ordered beverages and snacks, perhaps Eric slipped the drug into George's drink and then followed him back to the cemetery, where, after he was positive George was dead, stole the artifact. I know you believe this is far-fetched, Ed, but I'm on Annie's side. It can't hurt to interview Eric. The best-case scenario is that you'll rule him out as a suspect. I'm curious as to why you seem to be stonewalling this."

"That family has been through so much, Carrie, that I don't want to put them through anything more. Lily works from home. She's going to be uncomfortable with my interviewing Eric as a suspect."

Annie, impatient, argued, "I get it, Ed, but surely she'd want to know if her husband killed her father. If he didn't, then that's one more suspect to cross off the list. You're a masterful interviewer, it's one of your strongest skills, and I have complete confidence that you can figure out a way to talk with Eric Klein without anyone in that family believing you think he killed George. You have nothing to lose."

Ed threw up his hands in defeat. "The two of you aren't going to let up until I interview Eric, are you?"

Carrie and Annie grinned at each other.

"I concede. I'll call him this evening."

Chapter 51

The next morning Ed drove to Brighton to interview Eric Klein. The professor's only class that day was at 2:00; he'd be at home until after lunch. Despite Annie and Carrie's insistence, Ed didn't believe for an instant that the man had anything to do with George's death.

The Klein family lived on Greentree Road, a tree-lined street with gracious homes built in the 1930s and 40s. Ed parked in front of a sprawling stone and wood-sided two-story, landscaped in the front with yews, rhododendrons and azaleas. A lush green lawn bisected by a brick walkway led to the front door. No sports car was parked outside, a detached garage at the back of the property apparently housed the family's vehicles.

He rang the bell. Eric greeted him barefooted and wearing jeans and a black tee shirt with a silhouette of Abraham Lincoln outlined in white.

"Welcome." The men shook hands and Eric ushered Ed into a wide foyer with closets on each side and a wide stairway beyond that ended at a landing with a stained-glass window before continuing to the second floor. To the left of the foyer was a living room; behind it, the dining room, and to the right, a family room and study. The kitchen spanned the entire back of the house.

"I've been working at the kitchen table on a project; we can talk while I work. Can I get you anything to drink?"

"I'd appreciate a glass of water with no ice, please," Ed responded. The lanky college professor, who sported a short beard and a ponytail, ambled over to the refrigerator, opened it and poured water from a pitcher into a tall glass while Ed glanced at his notes.

"Ed, what can I do for you? You mentioned wanting to speak with me about the last conversation I had with George on the day he died."

"Yes. I'm trying to understand the sequence of events, Eric. Carrie Ramos, our police chief, indicated George called you that morning."

"He did, on my cell phone while taking a walk, about 10 a.m. He wanted the kids and me to come to Lighthouse Cove for an early dinner after Lily and Sally got back from Skaneateles, but the timing wasn't going to work, and I declined.

"I had no classes but did have a meeting late morning with some of my students at The Roasted Bean—it's a coffee shop in the student union. I dropped Jack off at my parents on my way but had to pick him up by 4:00 and then get Lexi from soccer practice, plus it was a school night for her."

"Did he say anything about finding something at the cemetery?"

"No, but I couldn't really talk because I was in the middle of the meeting. He understood. Now I regret cutting him off. Little did I know it would be the last time I'd speak with him."

Curious, Ed asked, "What were you meeting about?"

"My area of expertise is the Civil War, and we were planning a field trip to visit Underground Railroad sites in Wayne County for later in the fall or even possibly next spring."

That explains the tee-shirt, Ed thought. "Do you know much about the War of 1812?"

"Probably not much more than anyone else. Why?"

"We believe George's death is related to something he found at the cemetery where casualties of that war are buried. I'm not at liberty to say more. I'd like to speak to an expert on that period of history and hoped you'd be that person," Ed prevaricated.

Eric offered to provide Ed with a list of professors at the university and do a search for others in the Rochester area who might have that knowledge. He'd promised to email him with their contact information.

Ed thought about it before responding. Going through all the names and doing background checks would take time and be like looking for a needle in a haystack.

"No, that's okay. I appreciate the offer, but it probably would be a waste of your time and mine. I was chasing down a lead, but the more I think about it, I need to shift gears and go in a completely different direction."

Ed had downed his water and asked for a refill. As Eric walked back over to the refrigerator, he decided to bring up Eric's mother's health, it would appear he was making small talk.

"Eric, my wife, Annie, told me that Sally had indicated to her that your mother was having health problems. I hope it's nothing serious."

"Fortunately, it's not. At first, we thought she might be having heart problems, but it turned out to be an overactive thyroid condition. Iodine treatment and thyroid meds have put her right back on track. Thanks for asking."

"What about your dad, is he healthy?"

"He takes blood pressure medicine and a statin, that's just preventive. Although his cholesterol is slightly high, he's not had any heart issues and his doctor wants to keep it this way. I must admit I'm relieved both parents are relatively healthy. Losing George has been difficult, and I don't think our family could handle another death right now."

Ed was certain that Eric had had nothing to do with George's death. Just as he was about to end the interview, Lily walked into the kitchen.

"Oh, hi, Ed." She walked over to him and hugged him. "I understand you wanted to speak with Eric about my dad's death. I don't know what he can tell you that the rest of us haven't already shared. We're still having trouble understanding why he was murdered." Her eyes filled with tears.

"We all are, Lily. Frankly, I'm frustrated that it's been taking me so long to solve the case."

Lily was wearing a short, pale yellow tunic top over a pair of white leggings. Her only jewelry was a thin, gold wedding ring, small gold hoop earrings, and around her neck, a small antique-looking watch on a gold chain.

Noticing it, Ed remarked, "that's a beautiful watch; it must be quite old."

"Thanks. It is. A year ago, Eric spent a week at Gettysburg College as a guest lecturer. His parents watched the kids, and I went with him so we could do some sightseeing before we returned home. We found this at an antique shop, I fell in love with it, and he bought it for me as an early anniversary gift.

"Stay right there, I'll be back shortly." She left the room and within a minute returned with a paper. She laughed. "It even came with a certificate of authenticity. Here, look at this." She handed the paper to Ed. It verified that the watch had come from an estate of an old Gettysburg family, its provenance circa 1850s.

Ed trusted his instincts and as he examined the certificate, he started putting the disparate pieces of the investigation together. Then a tidal wave of certainty hit him, and he remembered what had drifted through his mind the morning he and Annie had viewed the cloisonné collection when they were in England.

Donna had explained that a pocket watch belonging to Robert Fitzhugh had gone missing from the collection. George, he was positive, had found that watch. And his killer must have believed Amanda had something in her possession related to it. What could that be? And why would someone kill an innocent man and attack an elderly woman for it?

Eric was not a suspect, still the visit had been productive. Ed admitted to himself that he'd wasted precious time chasing down false leads; now he could focus. His suspect, he was sure, was living in their community, had a heart condition and medical knowledge about how certain drugs can kill, and was quite knowledgeable about Lighthouse Cove's involvement in the War of 1812.

He ended the interview, and back in his car called Carrie first; then Annie to report his conclusions.

SUMMER
Chapter 52

Spring turned into summer with no additional threats to Amanda Reynolds' life and, thankfully, no additional murders, but also no leads. Ed and Carrie continued the investigation, but without Annie's input. The summer was the busy season for the museum with a steady stream of tourists and a myriad of activities.

She didn't have much free time this time of year, but Annie's interest in garden design and desire to learn more about the plants that could flourish in their northern climate prompted her to join the Lighthouse Cove Garden Club. Members of the club tended the village municipal gardens and pocket parks, took field trips and held classes about gardening techniques.

This year they'd also taken on the project of landscaping the cemetery after archaeologists had, to the best of their ability, reset the headstones and reburied the bones and shrouds that had surfaced after the early spring storms.

The annual meeting of the club was held in late June at The Olde Ballard Inn. The inn's restaurant overlooked its own splendid gardens, which members would tour before the lunch meeting. Annie provided transportation for Amanda; Eleanor had a doctor's appointment that morning and would arrive late.

The day was warm and sunny. After the meeting, Amanda invited her two friends to her house for a glass of lemonade. She directed them to a flagstone patio with a white cast iron bistro table and chairs overlooking the gardens while she went inside for the beverages, and a plate of lavender shortbread she'd baked that morning. Declining Annie's offer to help, she said her arthritis was much better, and she was able to walk the short distance without aid. Annie wasn't hungry, still she couldn't say no to her hospitable friend.

Old-fashioned and picturesque, the garden evoked the feeling of a bygone era. Bordering the property was a profusion of flowers that, when in full bloom later that summer, would look like a Monet painting.

While sipping and eating (and Annie and Eleanor waxing poetic over the shortbread), the women chatted amiably, and Amanda assured her friends that she was completely recovered from the attack and had received no additional threats. She asked Annie about her trip and reminisced about her own trips to England with her husband many years ago.

Annie told them about the Fitzhugh cloisonné collection and how one of the pieces—the pocket watch presumed to have been in Robert Fitzhugh's possession—had been lost. She explained that Ed believed George had discovered the watch the day he was killed, and that Amanda's attack had been related to it.

Amanda looked surprised; in fact, she seemed shocked. She admitted she was embarrassed she'd been unaware of the collection. She and her late husband had met with Fitzhugh relatives for dinner one night during a trip to London many years ago; no one had mentioned it and nothing about it had shown up in her research. Annie pulled out her phone and showed them the photos she'd taken of the collectibles.

Eleanor was expected in Williamson to look after her grandchildren and left a few minutes before Annie, who realized it was time to get back to the museum.

She thanked Amanda and promised her she'd be back to visit soon. Amanda seemed content sitting in the garden; Annie told her she'd see herself out.

Walking through the living room, she noticed how harmonious it appeared. Sunlight streamed through the wide mullioned windows that faced the street. Comfortable furniture, antique Oriental rugs worn to a silky sheen lay on oak floors, colorful knickknacks and paintings she assumed had been passed down through generations created a peaceful and pleasant ambience.

The floor to ceiling bookshelves on one wall caught her eye, and she stopped for a minute to view the reading material. She noticed a wide selection of books including the one Amanda had written about her ancestor, others on gardening and herbal medicines, and an impressive selection of classics, mysteries and biographies.

Amanda walked into the room just as Annie was heading for the front door. "Oh, Annie, I thought you'd left. You startled me."

"I'm afraid I got caught up in admiring this room, Amanda. It's charming. You must think of me as a real busybody, but I couldn't help but notice your vast selection of books. It's quite a collection."

"Is there anything that's of special interest to you, dear? I'm always happy to lend a book to a friend."

"No, thanks. I noticed the book you wrote and others I'm assuming you must have used to do research for it and realized that we've been so distracted lately that I completely forgot to tell you something. When Ed and I stopped in Sackets Harbor this spring on our way to Gananoque, I picked up a reproduction copy of a book that Morgan Lewis wrote. I believe he was an ancestor of yours. Are you aware of it?"

Amanda looked puzzled. "Lewis was related to Robert Fitzhugh, not on my side of the family, and his book doesn't sound at all familiar to me. I'm so embarrassed that I didn't know about it or the cloisonné collection. Have you read it?"

"I started it; quite frankly it's pretty boring, I have enough on my plate at present, and I haven't even mentioned it to Jason. He seems to be moving ahead nicely with the brochure without it. I'm not going to finish it, at least not right now. Would you like to borrow it? The docent at the gift shop at the museum in Sackets Harbor told me that it's out of print, and I bought the last copy."

"Why, yes, dear, I would. Hopefully nothing in it will change the facts of my own book about my ancestor. That would be terrible. How long may I keep it?"

"Keep it as long as you wish, Amanda. Call me after you're finished, and I'll come and get it."

Annie looked at her watch. She needed to get back to work, and after apologizing again to Amanda for startling her and perhaps overstaying her welcome, Annie promised to drop the book off the next day and to keep in touch.

Chapter 53

Fourth of July was even busier than Memorial Day in Lighthouse Cove. The days were long and warm, and tourists descended upon the village, renting cottages and staying at quaint inns and bed and breakfasts. When Annie contemplated retiring, it was usually at this time of year. She got little sleep and was perpetually exhausted from the abundance of activities that the museum sponsored.

Volunteers had helped to coordinate a 5K race, sailboat regatta, a large arts and crafts show, two concerts on the bluff. They had staffed a food truck that sold a variety of sandwiches, snacks and drinks, proceeds to benefit the museum. There was no admission charge to tour the museum over the holiday; crowds took advantage of guided tours and walked to the top of the lighthouse tower where, on a clear day, one could see all the way to Oswego, more than 30 miles to the east.

Henri and Eve Beauvoir typically hosted an annual cookout at their home on the night of the boat parade and fireworks display but decided this year instead to help Annie with the museum's many activities that wouldn't end until late afternoon. With concurrence from the DeCleryks and other friends, they reserved the top deck of Steelhead's—a new, modern bayside restaurant with a fabulous view, beyond, of the lake. Its brick oven spewed out delectable gourmet pizzas and other innovative and mouthwatering dishes.

The DeCleryk's children and grandchildren travelled from Rochester; Ed's Navy buddies and their families showed up, as did Suzanne and Garrett and for a short while, Carrie, Matt and their daughter, Natalya. Carrie's pregnancy was showing, and everyone congratulated the family on the anticipated new arrival.

Annie had invited Amanda, but she'd begged off. The high humidity seemed to make her arthritis worse, and the steps up to the deck would pose a challenge. She had decided to spend the evening across the bay at her friend Eleanor's house, where she could watch the fireworks from her patio.

Sally Wright joined the group for drinks but informed them she wasn't planning to stay for dinner or the other festivities, instead she would be traveling to Brighton to spend the evening with her family. Before leaving, she pulled Ed aside. As Samir had predicted, she remembered the threatening note George had received when they were living in Boston. Ed summarized his interview with Averill and subsequent meeting with Samir Abadi. He assured Sally that George's murder had nothing to do with his position at the Agency or his support of Alex Pulcov, now known as Peter Rigby.

Annie walked with Sally to her car, which was parked a block away. She wanted to have a few minutes alone with her friend to see how she was doing.

"I have something to tell you," Sally confessed. She said that remaining in Lighthouse Cove without George had become difficult; there were too many memories. She had purchased a condo in Brighton and would be moving into it by September. Determined to keep Windy Bluff in the family to honor the Wright family legacy, she had deeded the historic home to Lily and Eric who would spend summers and weekends there with their children. When she was ready, she promised to visit.

Liz, she reported, was more communicative but still depressed, and Averill had become noticeably frail. They would be relocating to a continuing care facility near the rest of the family and had sold their beach cottage to a couple from Pennsylvania who had recently retired.

Annie was sad but reassured her friend that she understood why she'd made the decision. She was granted permission to tell Ed and their other friends.

At dusk, the group, sad that Sally wasn't with them, settled in to watch the antique boat parade on the bay, and after, the spectacular fireworks display. Ed regretted not completing the restoration on his own boat. He and Annie had planned to participate in the parade this year, but the investigation had taken precedence. *Maybe next year*, he thought.

Chapter 54

The constant frenzy of activity during summer months in Lighthouse Cove was exciting, but for Annie, also exhausting. After the craziness of the July 4th celebration, the DeCleryks looked forward to quiet time where they could get back to a semblance of normalcy and their evenings on the back porch drinking wine and enjoying the simple dinners that Annie prepared from the fresh, seasonal ingredients she'd purchased at local markets.

One evening, after enjoying glasses of a delicious local unoaked chardonnay and a light meal of homemade gazpacho, an assortment of sheep's milk cheeses and artisanal breads, followed by dishes of local blueberries and raspberries, Ed acknowledged his frustration at not being able to close George Wright's case.

"I seem to be out of options. I still believe George found the missing pocket watch, but I can't figure out who would have known about it and killed him for it. I feel like I've let Sally and her family down."

"I understand, Ed, of course you do. George's killer seems to have fallen down a crack in the earth. Still, I don't know what more you can do."

"I've been thinking about it, and there's one more avenue I want to explore. Jason's completed the 1812 brochure. Is he working on any other projects?"

"I was going to have him start writing the next in the series, Lighthouse Cove's involvement with the Underground Railroad. Why?"

"We know Amanda's version of the story of her ancestor and his role in saving our village, and I'm not doubting it, but I also remember you telling me that the only Fitzhugh descendants she's aware of live in England or possibly the mid-west. Instead of starting the next brochure right now, would you allow Jason to do a search for descendants of Fitzhugh or Morgan Lewis who might live in New York state? I don't think it would take very long."

"I'll ask him. If he's willing, he can put off starting the next project for a few days. Tell me what you're thinking."

"I'm thinking we were on the wrong track about George meeting up with someone at the restaurant. Instead, perhaps someone else was at the cemetery the day George was killed—possibly a Fitzhugh descendant who had learned about the pocket watch and was searching for it. George may have been at the wrong place at the wrong time."

Annie sighed. "That makes sense, but why digitalis? That's not a commonly used poison to kill people."

"That's true, Annie. Remember, though, that the afternoon we brainstormed, we talked about the possibility that the killer is a man with a medical background and perhaps a heart condition and...."

Annie interrupted. "Ed, poison is typically a woman's weapon. Why are you so sure the killer is a man?"

"Is there someone on your radar screen you think I should be interviewing, Annie?"

"I've thought about it, but no, I can't imagine any women in George's or Amanda's circle of friends wanting them dead. Mary Williams was your first suspect, and it got me thinking. I guess I'm reaching because I want the crimes to be solved."

"I'm never completely certain about anything, Annie. But Amanda described her attacker as male. I believe her, so for now that's the direction I plan on taking."

"That makes sense. I guess I'm just as frustrated and upset about the lack of progress as you and Carrie are."

"I think we stay the course, Annie. Anyway, to continue, what I believe is that George was at the cemetery and found the watch shortly before this person arrived. He may have been friendly at first, and George may have shown him what he'd discovered.

"Perhaps after recognizing that the object as the one he was seeking, the person explained he was a descendant of Robert Fitzhugh, the owner of the watch, and requested that George give it to him. George may have resisted and informed him he was going to turn it over to the historical society. If the man was truly who he said he was and had a legitimate claim to the watch, he could contact you.

"He may have indicated he had no problem doing that, and after receiving your contact information, offered to stay and help George clean up the cemetery. It was warm that day, so maybe after a while he said he was going to take a break and get them cold beverages at one of our local eating establishments. Before returning to the cemetery, he slipped the drug into George's drink. Remember, there was that sports car we couldn't identify, perhaps it belonged to the killer."

"What about Amanda? Why would he go after her?"

"Donna indicated the watch opened in the back where a message could be placed. Maybe after stealing it, the killer found one that referred to another relic or something interesting about the Fitzhugh family. He may have recognized her name and that, unbeknownst to her they were related, and he mistakenly believed she was in possession of it.

"He must have been stalking her, remember she said she'd had hang-up calls for several days before she was attacked. He knew she had gone out for the morning and broke into her house to look for whatever he believed she had in her possession. She came home earlier than expected. He may have hidden then decided to attack and poison her to continue his search. Jason's arrival must have startled him and to avoid detection, he escaped through the back door.

"After she came home from the hospital she checked; nothing was missing, and that may be why she's received no additional threats. The killer didn't find what he was looking for."

Chapter 55

Jason had taken a couple weeks off to spend time with his family but was expected back that morning. He walked into Annie's office just as she had finished meeting with a couple docents.

"I'm glad to see you, Jason. How are you?"

Smiling broadly, Jason replied, "Great! My sister and her husband and baby came from Syracuse to visit; we attended some festivals in Rochester and even rented a pontoon one morning and went out onto the bay in Irondequoit."

"How's your dad?"

"That's even better news," Jason responded, looking visibly relieved, his brown eyes shining. "He's improving rapidly and with rehab, medicine and a change in diet, he should be able to live a fairly normal life. He'll have to get enough rest, exercise regularly and watch his stress level. He'll also need to take statins and blood pressure meds, but his doctor said he could return to work in September.

"We also contacted my doctor, and I had a full workup. For now, I'm fine, but because my dad's condition is genetic, I'll need to be checked every six months. I'm okay with that, my doctor assured me that there are lots of preventive measures we can take to make sure I stay healthy."

"Jason, that's wonderful!" Annie responded as she jumped up from her desk to give him a hug. "I know you were terrified, maybe now you can relax and try and enjoy the rest of the summer."

"I can, and I will. My mom has decided to work full-time. She loves what she's doing and said we'll save the extra money to safeguard for any future problems. I know she didn't want me to drop out of school; now I don't have to."

Jason told Annie he was ready to begin writing the brochure on the Underground Railroad; Annie explained that she'd like him to hold off on that. If he were willing, she wanted him to do some research on the Fitzhugh and Morgan Lewis families first. She mentioned Ed's belief that a descendant of Robert Fitzhugh might be involved in George's murder and Amanda Reynolds' attack and referred to the book she'd discovered in Sackets Harbor on the War of 1812.

"I decided not to mention it to you because you really didn't need to read it to complete your own research. It looked so boring to me that I didn't read it either, so I have no idea what's in it, but Lewis may have named family members with descendants living in this area. It might be a place for you to start. I loaned the book to Amanda. I'll call her and ask to get it back from her. Even if she's started but not finished it, she'll cooperate. She wants the case to be solved as much as the rest of us do."

"Of course, I'll help you."

"Thanks. I'll call her in a few minutes. I guess a place to begin would be to write down the names of those he mentions and then do an internet search for anyone living here in New York who might be related to them."

"I like challenges, Annie. I'll read the book and then start the project. Hopefully I'll find out something that will help Ed with his investigation."

Chapter 56

Annie called Ed, reporting that Jason was onboard and would begin the project as soon as she retrieved Morgan Lewis' book from Amanda; then she called her friend.

"Hello, Amanda. It's Annie. I hope you'll understand, but I'm going to have to get the Morgan Lewis book back from you this afternoon. I decided that perhaps Jason should read it. If we're lucky he'll find people named in it whose descendants live in the area who could be possible suspects in George's murder and your attack."

"Oh, my, Annie, I was just about to call you. I had an accident and...."

Annie interrupted. "Are you okay? Should I call 911?"

"Oh, no, dear, I'm fine, but something terrible has happened. I had planned to begin reading the book today. I didn't want to keep it for too long and had placed it on the table in the garden. I went inside to get myself a cup of tea and just as I reached the garden, I tripped on a pebble and fell against the table. The cup and saucer went flying and broke into smithereens right on the book. It's ruined, I'm so sorry."

Annie shook her head. "You're positive you're okay? Do you need medical attention?"

"I don't; I'm just a little bruised is all. I can call the gift shop in Sackets Harbor and order another copy of the book."

"No other books are in print, Amanda. Remember I mentioned that?" Annie was concerned. Could Amanda be suffering the beginning stages of dementia or had she just not paid attention when Annie had informed her that she had purchased the last copy.

Amanda didn't respond for a few seconds, then acknowledged, "That's right. I completely forgot. Now I'm even more distressed."

Nothing could be done about it. If Annie and Ed hadn't visited Sackets Harbor in the first place, she wouldn't have purchased the book, so no harm no foul. They'd have to move on with the investigation without it; an accident was an accident.

Reassuring Amanda that the book wasn't that important to the investigation and that she was glad she wasn't injured, Annie hung up. Hopefully the internet search would yield the information they were looking for.

Chapter 57

The phone rang immediately after Annie ended her conversation with Amanda and was starting towards Jason's office. *Oh dear, this day is certainly not going the way I want it to,* she thought. She answered it and was delighted to hear Suzanne's voice on the other line.

Suzanne asked Annie to join her for a walk around lunch time. The timing worked, and Annie suggested they walk to the beach. She would enjoy catching up with Suzanne; they hadn't spent any time alone since before she and Ed had gone to England.

"We can get sandwiches and drinks at the Gull Shack and sit under the pavilion where it will be cooler, while we eat them. I'll bring Gretchen and let her off leash. She likes to run and explore at the water's edge. She'll happily bark at the waves but would never in a million years go into the water." Annie laughed.

Instead of climbing the stairs to his office, Annie called Jason on the intercom and informed him that the Morgan Lewis book had been accidentally destroyed. He was disappointed but responded that he'd be fine conducting the research without it.

He opened his computer. After several minutes, he found an article from the Oswego daily newspaper written three years earlier about a doctor, Francis Livingston Lewis, aged 72, who had retired. It stated he was a direct descendant of Morgan Lewis, Quartermaster General for Western New York during the War of 1812. Bingo! He printed it out, and with it in hand walked downstairs to show Annie. She was just getting ready to leave to collect her friend, but excited, called her indicating she'd be a few minutes late. She wanted to read the article and knew she wouldn't enjoy her walk until her curiosity was satisfied.

"Jason, this might be the lead we're looking for. Excellent work! I'll call Ed and let him know about it."

Annie called Ed and read the article to him. He, too, was excited and planned to contact Carrie as soon as he and Annie ended their call. Hopefully they'd be able to get a search warrant that afternoon and before evening have a suspect in custody.

Chapter 58

At the same time Ed and Annie were speaking, Carrie was sitting in her office reading the *Rochester Area Police Digest* when Mia arrived for their daily morning meeting. She handed her boss a sealed envelope with Carrie's name on it in cut-and-pasted letters that appeared to have been clipped from a magazine.

"Barbara asked me to give this to you. She was so busy this morning after she first came in that she completely forgot." She explained that the receptionist had discovered it on her desk with a note from the night dispatcher who indicated that, after taking a quick coffee break last evening, he'd found it on the floor under the mail slot.

"Even though we lock the doors at night, whomever delivered this certainly could have rung the bell. I wonder why they didn't?"

Carrie shrugged. "Maybe they were in a hurry. Let me open this and see what's in it then we can have our meeting."

Inside, on a piece of computer paper, a message had been constructed with letters that appeared to have been cut from the same magazine: *For clues to finding your killer and who attacked Amanda Reynolds, look to Dr. Francis Livingston Lewis from Oswego.*

"Hmm, maybe my press conference finally bore fruit."

She handed Mia the note to read. "I don't want to hold you up, let's get this meeting out of the way, and then I'm going to call Ed. This may be the person who murdered George. A doctor certainly would understand how to administer a fatal dose of a potentially dangerous drug, and an aging doctor might have a heart condition and carry that drug with him. Maybe he owns that sports car we know was parked near the cemetery the day George was killed."

Several minutes later, she picked up the phone and dialed Ed's number.

"Hi, Carrie," Ed answered, recognizing her voice. "What a coincidence. I was just about to call you. What's up?"

She read him the note. "I'm cautiously optimistic, Ed. This might be the break we need."

"It gives credibility to what I just learned from Annie." He summarized the contents of the newspaper article Jason had found online.

The pair agreed that between the two new pieces of information, they may have found their killer.

"It's actually serendipitous, Carrie, that Jason found the article. Annie called Amanda to get the Morgan Lewis book back from her. Unfortunately, she said she had tripped and fallen, carrying a cup of tea that spilled on it. It's destroyed; we can't use it for research on possible names of descendants."

Ed paused for a few seconds than asked, "Why do you think the writer of the message chose not to identify him or herself?"

"Who knows? I dusted for prints, and there weren't any; apparently, he thought he'd be safer remaining anonymous. In any case, we need to follow up on it. I'm going to call the police chief in Oswego, Tim Owens. We've met a few times at conferences. Since we'll be in his jurisdiction, I want to make sure we bring him into the loop.

"I'll ask that he verify that Lewis is still living in Oswego, and if he is, request he get a search warrant. I expect he'll be able to get one fairly quickly."

"Any idea of when we'll be going?"

"Hopefully after lunch. I'll call you as soon as I have more information."

"Thanks. I'll call and give Annie a heads up."

Chapter 59

Annie was eager to tell Suzanne about her conversation with Ed. She collected her friend and they headed with Gretchen to the beach.

"Good news," she said. "We may have found George's killer."

She summarized the newspaper article about Francis Lewis and the tip Carrie had received. Carrie was contacting the police chief in Oswego to obtain a search warrant, and she and Ed were hoping to interview the suspect that afternoon.

"Cross your fingers that by this evening the case will be solved, and the person who killed George and attacked Amanda will be in custody. Ed's been a bit discouraged about the lack of progress, and I can't even begin to imagine what this is doing to Carrie. She's exhausted from the pregnancy."

"That's encouraging, Annie. It would be wonderful for everyone, especially the Wright family, to have some closure. I'll cross my fingers."

Annie, in the meantime, had noticed a round diamond surrounded by small sapphires set in a platinum band on her friend's left ring finger. She picked up Suzanne's hand and examined it. "Speaking of fingers, is this what I think it is?"

Suzanne grinned. "Yes, it is. Garrett proposed this weekend, and I accepted. It was a complete surprise That's partially why I wanted to spend time with you today. I wanted to tell you about it."

"Congratulations!" Annie hugged her friend. "We all adore him. I'm delighted for both of you and want to hear all the details."

Suzanne explained. Her mother had invited them to have lunch with the family on Sunday afternoon in the private banquet room of the restaurant her parents owned. The pair had plans to go to a concert in Rochester the night before; she was staying in the city for the weekend; the timing worked. She checked with Garrett and then called her mother back indicating they'd be there.

"Then what happened?" Annie asked.

"Something I never expected," Suzanne responded.

They hadn't seen Garrett's parents in a while, and Suzanne thought it might be nice to invite them for an early breakfast on Sunday morning.

"Garrett reminded me that we had to be at the restaurant no later than noon, but I insisted. I really like his parents and was disappointed when they said they had other plans. Instead, we walked to a local deli, purchased bagels, lox and a copy of *The New York Times* and went back to his condo where we spent a relaxing morning until it was time to go."

"What happened next?" Annie prompted.

"This is where it gets really good. We walked into the restaurant, and not only were my parents and siblings there with their families, but also Garrett's parents and his two sons from his first marriage. They yelled 'Surprise!'. I had no idea why. It wasn't either of our birthdays. I was puzzled.

"Then Garrett dropped to his knees, pulled a velvet box out of his pocket and opened it and said, 'Before all those who mean the most to us, I profess my love to you, Suzanne Gordon, for now and always. Will you marry me?'"

Annie, delighted, responded, "Well, that's certainly one of the most creative proposals I've ever heard about."

"Yes, I was pretty stunned and at first didn't know whether to be angry or exuberant. I decided to be the latter. I realized it was completely in character for him, wanting our families to be part of it. I'm forty-five and never planned to marry, but I love the guy and can't imagine life without him. We'll have to work out the details of our living arrangements, but Rochester is not far from here, and we can probably manage to keep both places. I think life with him is going to be just grand."

Annie reached up to hug her dear friend. They all needed happy news for a change.

From the Letters of Rebecca Fitzhugh

December, 1816
My dear sister, Marigold,

I write to you with a heavy heart. As we prepare to celebrate the day of our Savior's birth, which should be both joyous and festive, I am distressed beyond belief. Robert is indeed a traitor, but to the United States; not England. During his time in New York he served as a double agent, working with the British during the war to further their goal of achieving victory in our new country.

Two mornings ago, Patience and Charity implored me to take them to visit their Aunt Felicity, Robert's sister. She lives with her husband and their three children on a nearby estate, and my girls have become quite fond of their cousins. Their governess and tutor had been given leave to visit their families for the holidays, and I was striving to entertain the children and keep them occupied, thus a visit to Felicity seemed to be in order. They implored me to ask their Papa to join us.

Robert was meeting with his father in his study that morning, and I repaired there to ask him to join us. The door was closed, but I heard the two speaking in hushed tones. I feel ashamed to admit I stayed outside and eavesdropped.

They were discussing the children and me, and my father-in-law indicated how pleased he was that we had adapted easily to our new country and that the children were flourishing. He admitted he was grateful to the

King for being willing to go along with the ruse to spare me the embarrassment of knowing the truth. I was puzzled, then moved away from the door and without asking my husband to join us, took the children to visit with their aunt and cousins, where we spent a delightful afternoon. Still, their conversation disturbed me.

Later that evening after we had retired to our chambers, I questioned Robert, confessing to what I had heard. At first, he laughed. I had misunderstood the conversation, he replied. But I pressed on, asking what his father had meant about the King and promised there would be no rest for either of us until he told me the truth. And then what he confessed completely shattered my belief that Robert is an honest and honorable man.

As you are aware, Robert's cousin Morgan Lewis had invited Robert to emigrate to New York to serve as one of his aides when he was governor. At the time, relationships between our two countries were peaceable. Months later, when the war commenced and Cousin Lewis was named Quartermaster General of Western New York, he asked Robert to remain on his staff, this time to help the U. S. win the war.

Shortly after, Robert received a confidential message from King George requesting he serve as a double agent, providing information he'd learned from Lewis to British spies who were now residing in western New York. I was shocked when he confessed that he had never fully adapted to his life in America and after days of consideration sent word to the King that he would accept his request and assist his country of birth.

His father had, all along, been aware of his mission but was distressed when Robert returned to England without the children and me, as he had vowed to bring us with him after the war had ended and it was safe to do so. Robert told his father that one of our militiamen had overheard him speaking to a British agent, shortly after a couple ships in the flotilla anchored in Silver Bay to provision.

During that discourse, Robert learned that the British soldiers intended to burn many of the buildings and homes in our village, and despite his fealty to England was bitterly opposed; he and the agent fought about it. In the end, Robert conceded he had no power to stop it. The agent promised that our home would not be destroyed, and he kept his promise.

That afternoon in the woods, near what is now the cemetery where our patriots are buried, the militiaman confronted Robert about what he'd overheard. There was an altercation and during it Robert's coat was torn.

Robert ran from the site and believes that the militiaman took his bejeweled pocket watch which he discovered was missing later that evening. It had probably fallen from his pocket. Perhaps the militiaman planned to use it as evidence against Robert; Robert never knew.

Given the circumstances, the soldiers, after completing their mission later that evening, had no choice but to take my husband with them. They captured two more militiamen but released them at Oswego, indicating they had no space on the ship for additional prisoners of war. The patriots were told that Robert, who had been a British subject, would be transported with them, tried for treason and hanged.

But truth be told, Robert was a free man the second he stepped onto the ship. The story that the King had pardoned him was a sham to spare me the knowledge that Robert was not a traitor to his own country but to ours.

I fear, dear sister, that our marriage was merely one of convenience for Robert to gain respectability in our village. I am not sure he ever truly loved me, and it grieves me sorely to admit it, although he insists that I am gravely mistaken. We had earlier resumed our marital relations, and I am again with child.

After the babe is born, I shall return with my three children to New York. Robert has been quite generous, and I am in the possession of several pieces of jewelry I can sell for currency, plus I have managed to save for emergencies, such as this. I cannot and will not stay with him, but I will confront him and explain that I am leaving because I disdain his treachery and can no longer trust him.

My lady's maid has posted this for me as I fear it would not be sent otherwise.

I remain your loving sister,
Rebecca

Chapter 60

The police chief in Oswego had been extremely cooperative and executed a warrant that the judge reluctantly signed, indicating he knew of the well-regarded family and cautioned that they treat Dr. Lewis with respect.

Carrie called Ed. "I'll pick you up in five minutes, and we'll meet Chief Owens at his station and then go together to the Lewis house."

An hour later, the three investigators arrived at 238 Willow Street. The stone and frame Dutch Colonial-style home was set back from a yard with two mature Japanese maple trees flanking a stone walk that ended at three steps leading up to a front door, painted soft yellow. A gray Ford minivan was parked in the attached portico to the right of the home, but no sports car. Perhaps Dr. Lewis had taken it out for a drive.

Chief Owens rang the bell, and a tall, gray-haired woman, who appeared to be in her mid-to-late 60s, appeared at the door. She was wearing ivory linen slacks, a light blue silk shirt and silver sandals. Owens introduced himself, Carrie and Ed, then presented his badge and the search warrant.

"Are you Mrs. Lewis, the wife of Dr. Francis Lewis?"

The woman looked alarmed. "Yes, I am Clarissa, Francis' wife. Is this about my husband?"

Chief Owens replied, "We'd like to come inside, Mrs. Lewis. We're investigating a murder, and we have reason to believe your husband might know something about it." He decided not to mention the attack on Amanda, hoping that in time the rest of the story would reveal itself.

Clarissa laughed. "This must be a very bad joke. Our newspaper carried the story of the murder; that was a while ago. I can't imagine why you would believe Francis would know anything about such a heinous crime."

No one answered; she took a deep breath. "Oh, my, you think he's the murderer, don't you?" She laughed. "That's simply preposterous; you can't begin to imagine why."

Tim Owens replied, "I think we'll be the ones to determine that, ma'am."

She started to argue with him. Ed interrupted, "Does he happen to have a heart condition?"

Puzzled at the question, Clarissa answered warily, "He does, along with many other physical ailments. Why?"

"Is digitalis one of his drugs?"

"It is, but I don't understand who could have informed you that he could be involved in a crime like this. It's impossible. Please, let me explain…."

Ed interrupted her again. "We had an anonymous tip, Mrs. Lewis. We noticed a Ford minivan in your driveway. Do you or your husband also happen to own a sports car?"

"No," she responded impatiently. "We have one car, the one that's under our portico."

Ed and Carrie looked at each other. They were thinking the same thing: *The additional set of tire tracks belonging to a sports car may have had nothing to do with George's murder. In that case, perhaps Lewis had parked his car elsewhere and hiked to the cemetery, or, as they earlier suspected, the men had met at The Cove.*

"We'd still like to speak with your husband; we have a few questions. Is he here?"

"He's at a doctor's appointment, our daughter is with him. He should be back shortly, but I can assure you, you aren't going to get much out of him."

Clarissa Lewis reluctantly allowed the investigators into her home and removed herself to the study. Pulling on gloves and booties, they began their search, spreading throughout the house, hoping to find evidence that could tie Lewis to the crimes. Within minutes, Ed discovered a cloisonné pocket watch lying on a sideboard in the dining room.

He called out, "Hey Carrie, Tim, can you come into the dining room? I think I found what we've been looking for." The pair arrived within seconds, and he held up the watch.

Carrie grinned and gave Ed a thumb's up. The police chief high-fived him. On the trip from the police station to the Lewis home, Ed had summarized his and Annie's trip to England where they had viewed the Fitzhugh cloisonné collection and learned about the missing pocket watch; the family's relationship to the patriot, Robert Fitzhugh; and Ed's belief that George had discovered the watch in the cemetery the day he was killed.

"We'll get our answers as soon as Dr. Lewis returns home," Ed remarked, "but perhaps the day the two men met, George shared that he had AFib and was taking a beta blocker.

"Mrs. Lewis has verified her husband has a heart condition. It's quite possible he carries digitalis with him, and being a doctor, he knew that combining it with the beta blocker would kill George and he could walk off with his prize."

Carrie remarked, "This doesn't appear to be a family in financial need; what other reason could there be for him to be so desperate to get it? Did he learn about the watch from family stories handed down from one generation to another or by reading his ancestor's book?"

"Unless Lewis has a copy of that book or is willing to be forthcoming about how he learned about the watch and why he was so desperate to get it, we may never know. Another possibility is that the answers lie in letters we believe Fitzhugh's wife wrote to her sister who lived in Pennington, after she'd emigrated to England. Those seem to have disappeared, but maybe Lewis believed Amanda has possession of them, and that's why he attacked her. For some reason, he may have believed they would reveal the existence of another artifact or expose some deep, dark family secret."

Chief Owens had been listening intently to the conversation and shook his head. Ed called Clarissa Lewis into the dining room and had just begun questioning her when they heard the front door open.

"Hi, mom, we're back," a female voice announced.

"I'm in the dining room, Kathy."

"Let me get dad settled, and I'll be right in," she responded.

Within a minute, the younger woman, who appeared to be in her mid-40s, entered the room, completely baffled at why three strangers, two of them dressed in police uniforms, were with her mother.

Clarissa explained who they were and what they suspected, and Kathy, like her mother, laughed. It was harsh and unpleasant. "You believe my father was involved in a murder? That's impossible. Please, follow me." She motioned them toward the living room.

On a recliner sat a man staring into space. He was in his mid-70s but looked at least twenty years older, with thinning hair and age-spotted hands that trembled even as he held them on his lap. He had a vacant look in his eyes.

He glanced at his wife. "Are you my nurse?" He looked at his daughter. "Or are you my nurse? Or are you my wife? I don't understand."

Clarissa took his hand and, with love and compassion in her eyes, responded patiently, "Dear, I'm your wife, Clarissa, and this young woman is your daughter, Kathy. She just took you to see the doctor and now you're back at home."

Dr. Lewis replied, "Oh, yes, that's right. Sometimes I just forget." He sighed and lowered his head to stare at his lap.

Clarissa Lewis looked at Carrie, Ed and Chief Owens and explained, "You can't possibly have the right person. My husband is suffering from advanced Lewy Body dementia. I normally have 'round the clock care for him. His caregiver had the day off; today my daughter is helping me out.

"Francis does not recognize me or our children. He can barely speak and can hardly walk. He has a heart condition and many other ailments. We administer all his drugs; he's incapable of doing it for himself. I'm sorry to hear about the murder and hope you find the person who did this. It's not my husband."

Chapter 61

Ed was shocked. Dr. Lewis couldn't possibly be the killer, still, he had questions about the watch.

"I'm terribly sorry to have intruded on you, Mrs. Lewis, this must have been upsetting. I understand now that your husband couldn't be our murderer, but I believe someone in your family may have been." He held up the watch.

"A cloisonné pocket watch, dating back to the early 1800s matching this description, was missing from a collection in England. We think it was accidentally buried with a casualty of the War of 1812 at a cemetery in Lighthouse Cove. Please explain how you came to be in possession of it."

"This is not the watch you're looking for, Mr. DeCleryk. An anonymous giver sent it to us."

Clarissa proceeded to explain that a few days earlier they had received a package in the mail. It required her signature which puzzled her. She had ordered nutritional supplements from an online drug outlet and without paying attention, thought it was those that were being delivered. She opened the package and inside was the watch. The return address on the package was from a jeweler in Wisconsin, who had placed a business card inside the package. There was no indication of who sent the watch, only a computer-generated note saying, "Surprise! This is for making my day. Enjoy!"

She continued, "I'd hoped that whomever purchased the watch would call and admit to it and explain why they had sent it. After a couple of days, when no one did, I called the jeweler hoping she would identify the sender. I wanted to thank that person; the watch is lovely.

"She said the sender had discovered the watch on her website and the transaction occurred through an email request followed by a cashier's check from a national bank. No return address was on the envelope that the check and message came in, and she didn't pay attention to the postmark. She agreed the situation was odd and she wondered about the sender's motive, but there was nothing about the watch that would harm anyone, so she sent it.

"After receiving notice from the post office that the watch had been delivered and that they had my signature, the jeweler deleted the email. She remembered it was from a Gmail account with an odd username: numbers, letters and symbols instead of the account holder's name. She expected we'd call her if the item arrived damaged."

Clarissa Wright continued, "The piece appeared to be an antique, but I wasn't certain. When I questioned its authenticity, I was assured the watch was merely an accurate reproduction."

"I have no idea how we got in the middle of this. I fear that, for whatever reason, you've been purposely misled. I discarded the package it came in but kept the jeweler's business card; you're welcome to call her. She'll confirm what I've just told you." She handed Ed the card.

The jeweler verified Clarissa's story. The investigators apologized to Mrs. Lewis and her daughter for intruding in their lives and upsetting them. Then Ed had a thought.

"Do you know anyone who might have a grudge against you and your husband?"

Clarissa Lewis shook her head. "I can't imagine anyone we know wanting to put us through this. Francis was a beloved family practitioner and never intentionally caused harm to anyone. We still get Christmas cards from some of his former patients. We're decent people, Mr. DeCleryk, who live a quiet life."

After apologizing again to Clarissa and her daughter, the trio got into Carrie's car and headed back to Chief Owens' office, feeling not only discouraged and frustrated, but also embarrassed and angry.

Carrie admitted, "I guess we didn't do our due diligence, and I feel awful. Whoever delivered the message to my office and sent that watch to the Lewis family played a terribly cruel joke on them. They have enough to deal with, given Dr. Lewis' dementia and other health issues."

"Carrie, without fingerprints we couldn't possibly identify the sender of the message you received, and the lead seemed solid," Ed responded. "Our killer is quite diabolical. His purpose for doing this was to put us off track and create yet another delay in our finding him."

Tim Owens commented, "I'm sorry it didn't work out, but you did the best you could under the circumstances. We all make mistakes, don't beat yourselves up about it."

"I'm more baffled than ever," Carrie said. "We keep running into obstacles, and we may yet again have hit a snag. George's killer and Amanda's attacker may never be caught."

Feeling fatalistic, they hoped there would be no additional casualties.

Chapter 62

Carrie and Ed dropped Tim Owens off at his office, thanked him for his cooperation and began their journey back to Lighthouse Cove. On their way out of town, they stopped at a gas station and while Carrie was using the restroom, Ed purchased a bottle of water for her and a bottle of iced tea for himself.

"Fresh from the vending machine," he smiled, as they clinked bottles. "Wish it could be stronger, but you're driving and pregnant and as much as I could use a drink right now, it's no fun drinking alone." He grinned, then asked, "How are you feeling? I didn't have a chance to ask you earlier."

"Much better, in fact, no more sickness and I'm not nearly as tired as I was. The baby's kicking, and he seems quite strong. We're calling him a him. I'm convinced I'm having a boy this time. We've even decided on a name, Arturo, after Matt's grandfather, who died a few years ago."

"I expect Matt's family will be very pleased with your decision. Now, let's talk about what happened today. I'm very discouraged and thinking maybe it's time to close the case. We've run out of leads, and I'm completely stumped about what to do next."

"I'm not closing it, Ed, but let's take a break for a while and let things settle. Maybe with a little distance we'll be able to come up with other ideas. I'm frustrated and angry that we're not making any headway."

Ed sighed. "Me, too. We're pretty sure the murder and attack are related to the watch I believe George found at the cemetery and someone's misguided belief that Amanda is in possession of something related to it. We have no other explanation. We've looked at all aspects of George's life and have come up with nothing. I'm beyond embarrassed at what we put Francis Lewis' wife and daughter through this afternoon. I wouldn't mind taking a break, and you may be right that a little distance will give us clarity to explore other possibilities.

"Speaking of breaks, Annie and I are having a brunch at our house this Sunday, starting at 11:00. Weather permitting, we'll eat outside on the porch. Are you, Matt and Natalya able to join us?"

"I'll have to check with Matt, but I think we'll be able to attend. Will other children be there? If not, we can get a sitter."

"No need to do that, Carrie. Our children and grandchildren from Rochester will be joining us, so there will be playmates for your daughter."

"She'll love that. What can we bring?"

"You'll have to talk with Annie, she's in charge of the menu. I'll ask that she call you."

Carrie thanked Ed, who after leaving her office headed home. He was looking forward to having a drink with Annie and sharing stories of their day; he suspected hers had gone better than his. While he was feeling regret that the case had not yet been solved, he admitted to himself that he was also somewhat relieved to be able to take a break from the investigation for a while. Summer went quickly on Lake Ontario, and he'd now have time to enjoy this bountiful season.

Chapter 63

I'm off the hook, the killer thought. I've led them on a wild goose chase, what fun! They'll feel like fools when they discover that Francis Lewis couldn't have possibly committed either the murder or assault on an elderly woman. That'll show them not to mess with me.

The killer laughed. This gets better and better with each day that passes. Once they realize their error, they'll be back to square one. They're never going to catch me; I'm way too smart for them and way too wily. For some reason if I'm wrong, and I'm rarely wrong, and they do figure it out, I know just what I'll do. It will just be another unfortunate consequence.

They'll be frustrated and exhausted, exactly what I'd hoped for. They'll be worn out and discouraged. All the better. This isn't over, not quite yet. One more must go, then all loose ends will be tied up. I could kill the investigators but killing them will just stir things up, then others would be brought in and the hunt would only intensify and call more attention to the crime.

Yes, I'll never get caught. Still, I'm getting tired of playing this game; I just don't have an appetite for it. I'm not going to obsess about it though. They'll never solve this. Ever. The killer chuckled. Boy, would they be surprised if they knew what was really going on.

Chapter 64

As Annie and Ed had hoped, Sunday dawned with a bright sky, low humidity and temperatures expected in the high 70s. The perimeter of their porch was crowded with flowers, herbs and vegetables that grew in large terra cotta pots on wheeled stands. From the ceiling hung smaller pots of brightly colored petunias. Comfortable wicker chairs, cushioned in vintage fabrics, had been placed in the yard, facing the water.

They had set metal chairs and small tables with French linens on the porch and in the yard. For centerpieces Annie had filled Mason jars with flowers from her garden. A long buffet table, covered in colorful printed fabrics, stood at one end of the porch.

The menu consisted of cold cucumber soup, Chinese chicken salad, Provencal tuna sandwiches, a pasta salad made with pesto, pignolia nuts and fresh peas, and a seasonal fruit platter. For dessert Annie had baked blueberry and raspberry tarts filled with lemon curd.

Guests would bring appetizers and additional desserts and help themselves to frosty pitchers of homemade Sangria, iced tea and water infused with lemon and lime wedges, chilled bottles of dry Rosé; an assortment of white wines and craft beer.

Their children and grandchildren arrived promptly at 11:00 a.m., then shortly after, Suzanne and Garrett; the Ramos' with daughter, Natalya; Ed's Navy buddies and their spouses and partners; their friends Henri and Eve.

Jonathan Bradford had accepted their invitation and introduced everyone to his date, Stephanie Morris. She was friendly and warm, and despite missing Emily, Ed and Annie hoped the relationship would become permanent.

Sally Wright had ventured out from Brighton. Most of those attending the brunch were her friends and delighted to see her. Ed had picked up Amanda Reynolds from her house, and the sprightly woman had dressed festively in a black caftan printed with huge red hibiscus flowers, gold sandals and a beach hat. She hadn't met Sally and upon learning she was present asked Annie to introduce them. She hugged her, admitting that although she'd not known George, she was terribly saddened for her loss.

Bocce, croquet and volleyball had been set up in the yard; however, most guests were content to sit and watch the gentle waves roll onto the beach below them and enjoy the lovely day, tasty food and relaxed camaraderie.

FALL
Chapter 65

The summer, as summers do, sped by quickly, with each weekend filled with a flurry of outdoor activity that would end in several weeks as snowbirds drove south, summer residents went back to the cities, and year-round residents prepared for the ensuing colder months.

Labor Day weekend arrived with temperatures in the low 80s. Streaks of white from jet contrails made patterns against the brilliant, clear azure sky as small white caps rolled up against the beach breaking through the soft, undulating teal blue sea.

The season ended with another round of picnics, concerts and sailboat regattas and a spectacular fireworks display. Annie looked forward to a respite after working non-stop over the past several months, and she and Ed agreed that despite the murder case not having been solved, they'd enjoyed participating in the multitude of activities that were held during warm weather in their village.

The museum closed for a few days after the last of the holiday weekend festivities. Jason returned to school, but Annie, pleased with how well he'd done over the summer, had offered him a part-time position that he could work around his classes.

Earlier in the spring, Amanda had committed to speaking to a group at the museum's monthly luncheon lecture series that began in September. On a bright, warm, sunny Thursday, Annie knocked on her door at

11:30 a.m. to drive her to the event. When her friend opened the door, she was surprised at how frail she had become in the few weeks since she'd last visited with her.

"Are you ill, Amanda? We can cancel your speaking engagement at the luncheon today."

"That's not necessary, Annie. It's just my age catching up with me. My arthritis is worse, and I'm having to rely more heavily on my cane and my walker. My blood pressure has always been quite low, and as a result I'm occasionally light-headed and frequently tired. My doctor says it's not life-threatening. I guess I'll just have to live with it. I can certainly speak this afternoon. Come in for a few minutes while I collect my purse and the materials I'll need for the talk."

Annie entered the house. She could see Amanda's garden through the dining room windows and remarked, now that it was in full bloom, how beautiful it was.

"Go ahead and take a look, dear, we have a few minutes."

Annie walked outside and smiled. She was able to recognize the purple salvia and lavender, red cone flowers, blue delphinium, black-eyed Susan, lily-of-the-valley, wild mint and a proliferation of other perennials, ablaze in glorious color. An arbor covered with wisteria and a wooden walkway led to another part of the yard where a pond filled with Koi rippled peacefully.

"This is lovely, Amanda. I knew this spring that the garden would be spectacular by late summer. I didn't imagine just how much."

"It is, but as I think you are aware, Annie, I didn't do the work, just supervised the man I've hired to maintain it for me. Unfortunately, my gardening days are behind me."

"I'm so sorry to hear that. I know how much you enjoyed puttering around."

"I did, but those days are over. I've also hired someone to clean my house for me. I just can't do it myself anymore. I'd love to be able to stay here, but it's becoming too difficult. I'm thinking of selling and moving into a senior resident center; it might make sense to do that soon."

Chapter 66

Ed's phone rang at 3:00 the next afternoon. It was Carrie. He had just completed a plan of action for a consulting job he'd scheduled for later that month with a police force in a town south of Buffalo.

"Hi, Carrie."

Without preamble, she announced, "There's been another death."

"A bar fight after hours last night in front of Captain Rick's end badly? Someone in a drunken stupor crash his boat?" he asked.

Carrie was impatient. "Ed, I wouldn't be calling you for something like that. It's bad."

Ed felt a stab of anxiety in his chest, "Who, then?"

"Eleanor Brown, Amanda's dear friend, was found dead in her home this morning."

"Oh, my. Was she murdered?"

"Possibly."

Carrie explained. Amanda had called the station around 10 a.m., expressing concern for her friend. She'd reported that the night before, she, Eleanor, and two others had gone for dinner and drinks at a pub on the water at Port Bay then to a movie in Wolcott that started at 8:00. Eleanor had driven, and she'd dropped Amanda off last, at about 10:45 and then, she believed, had driven directly home.

The same four women had agreed to meet at their church at 9:00 this morning for coffee and pastries and to organize for the upcoming fall harvest festival.

Everyone but Eleanor arrived a few minutes before the appointed time. The group socialized for a while, thinking she was running late. At 9:30, Eleanor still hadn't arrived; Amanda called her house. When she didn't answer her phone, Amanda assumed she was on her way. Fifteen minutes later, she'd still not arrived, and Amanda called her cell phone; again, there was no response. Alarmed, she called the police station. She feared that perhaps her friend had become ill and unable to answer her phone or had been in an accident. No accidents had been reported that morning.

Carrie sent Mia to check on her. The garage door was open, and Eleanor's car was parked inside. Mia rang the bell. When Eleanor didn't answer, she called Carrie, and the police chief suggested she try the door. She turned the knob, and it opened. She discovered Eleanor dead, face down in the foyer.

The medical examiner and an ambulance arrived within minutes of Carrie, and a short time later Mike reported that time of death appeared to be between 11:30 p.m. and 1:00 a.m. last night. He asked Carrie to contact next of kin. She explained to him that Mia had searched through the house and discovered photos that appeared to be of children and grandchildren, but no address book, and the contacts in Eleanor's cell phone were listed by first name only. She didn't know where to begin.

Carrie was hoping Amanda would be able to give them the information. But upon learning about her closest friend's death, she'd become hysterical and attempts to get answers to their questions had been unsuccessful.

Mike decided to conduct an autopsy and order a tox screen, proforma for someone who'd died without a family member present. He called Carrie back several hours later. As he suspected, Eleanor had been murdered. Her heart and other organs showed no sign of disease. She had traces of digitalis in her system along with other poisons he couldn't readily identify, and it would take time to figure out what they were. In addition to the poison, her stomach contents indicated food and alcohol, and he'd found receipts for the dinner and the movie in her purse, confirming Amanda's report of what had occurred the night before.

"This isn't making any sense, Carrie," Ed replied. "Why would anyone kill Eleanor Brown? We were pretty sure both George's murder and Amanda's attack were related to the pocket watch we believe George found at the cemetery. Eleanor's murder certainly changes things."

"Or maybe not, Ed. The killer wasn't successful at his attempt to murder Amanda and she's now protected by a security system. He must have realized that digitalis isn't necessarily fatal to healthy people and added other poisons as insurance. Maybe Eleanor's murder is a strong warning to Amanda to produce whatever it is he believes she's in possession of, or more will die. I'm going to order a tap on her phone in case he calls her."

"Amanda was clueless about why she'd been attacked, Carrie, and has no idea what her attacker wanted. Even if he calls and says what he wants, she may not have it."

"I know, Ed, and it's terribly puzzling, but it might help us identify the murderer. Amanda is a basket case, even several hours after learning about her friend's death. Mia is with her now, trying to calm her down. She's inconsolable, verging on hysteria. We need to question her about last night as soon as possible. Maybe she'll remember something that can help us figure out who killed Eleanor and at the same time give us the contact information for Eleanor's family."

Carrie paused. "Would Annie be willing to go over to her house and be with her for a while? Maybe her presence will help."

"Annie's at work. I'll call her, let her know what's going on. If she can break free, I'll ask her to meet us at Amanda's house."

From the letters of Rebecca Fitzhugh

March, 1817
My dear Marigold,

My babe, a boy, was born a fortnight ago, and he is a strong and healthy lad whom we've named Henry. As you are aware, I had planned to return to the United States as soon as he grew strong and able to travel with the girls and me.

Robert has implored me to stay. The conversation I related to you in my last letter continued for many days. He vowed that he had married me for love and had never intended for Lighthouse Cove to be burned when the British invaded our village. His guilt, he admitted, was more than he could bear, and he has begged me to forgive him.

After his successful escape from Lighthouse Cove back to England, he confessed he and his family had feared I would never be able to make the long journey with Charity and Patience to be with him. He'd been despondent with the knowledge that he had sacrificed his love for his family to honor his King. When he learned of my determination to make the trip to England and that we would be finally reunited, he was overjoyed.

I love Robert and always will, so for now we have made our peace with one another. He has pledged to find some way of earning my trust and devotion again, and I've pledged to stay with him and keep his children from learning of his deceit.

I trust you and Remington are enjoying a more tranquil life than I.
   Your loving sister,
   Rebecca

Chapter 67

Ten minutes later, Ed, Carrie and Annie arrived at Amanda's house. Hours earlier, after Eleanor's body had been transported to the morgue, the police chief had called the county sheriff's office to request they send criminal technologists to investigate the scene. After leaving Amanda, Mia returned to the house to assist them.

Amanda rushed into Annie's arms and sobbed, while her friend hugged her. After gulping a glass of water and taking several deep breaths, she seemed composed enough to talk.

"Are you sure you're okay, Amanda? I know you've suffered a horrible blow," Ed asked.

"What's happening in this village?" Amanda asked Ed, as she began to cry again. "Do you believe that Eleanor's death is related to George Wright's murder and my attack? Was she murdered?"

"Yes, she was, Amanda. She died from a fatal combination of digitalis and other poisons that Mike's not yet been able to identify."

"She was my dearest friend in the entire world," she wailed. "What a cruel thing to do."

"I realize how distressed you are," Ed responded, "but please think carefully. Can you remember anything that would help us find the person who did this?"

Amanda looked puzzled. "I've said this before. I have no idea why anyone would want to kill George Wright and attempt to murder me, and I certainly don't know why anyone would want to kill my dearest friend in the entire world."

"Here's what I'm thinking, Amanda," Ed responded. "George discovered Robert Fitzhugh's missing pocket watch—you know, the one Annie told you about? Inside it may have been a message. We believe George and the killer's paths crossed the day he was murdered, someone with medical expertise who may be living here in our community who killed George for the watch. He may be someone in your circle of friends and acquaintances, and aware of your background, believes you are in possession of something that could be damaging to him or his family, maybe even the missing letters Rebecca Fitzhugh wrote to her sister.

"We know what happened the day he broke into your home. If Jason hadn't arrived when he did, you might have died. Then, when you had the security system installed, you further foiled his plot. When you're out in public, you're always with friends. He can't get to you now. You need to be straight with me, Amanda. Have you received any threats, phone calls or letters that you haven't told us about? Threats that if you didn't give this person what he wanted, someone you cared about would die?"

Amanda pressed her lips shut, then spoke. "No, of course not. I certainly would have reported it if I had. I seem to remember telling you, or maybe it was Carrie, that I've had hang ups, I'm sure they were wrong numbers. I've received no threats. Whatever's going on has just caused me to lose my best friend. Please find this person and bring him to justice."

"We're trying to do that," Carrie responded. "We think Eleanor's death may be a warning to you and this person may try and get in touch with you. We'll tap your phone. If he calls, please try and keep him on the line as long as possible."

"I hope that doesn't happen," Amanda responded. "I don't know how much more of this I can take." She started crying again.

Carrie asked, "Was Eleanor in the habit of keeping her doors unlocked?"

Amanda dried her eyes with a tissue she'd taken from a pocket in her sweater and took a few deep breaths, trying to calm herself. "Yes, she was. After I was attacked, I begged her to install a security system, and to keep her doors locked. She was adamant her street was safe, and she had no reason to think her life was in danger. She only locked up at night before she went to bed; she didn't feel it was necessary any other time of the day. If she had, maybe she'd still be alive." She started crying again.

Ed and Carrie were completely stumped. Eleanor's murder was complicating things; they were at a loss about what to do about it.

Carrie's phone rang, it was Mia. The techs had found no additional clues that would help solve Eleanor's murder—no fingerprints, nothing seemed to be missing. Mia reported that while they had been investigating, she'd gone door-to-door and questioned the neighbors, no one had seen or heard anything out of the ordinary last night, no suspicious-looking cars or people who didn't belong there.

After ending the call, Carrie pressed Amanda for information about Eleanor's next of kin. Amanda replied that she'd been widowed years ago, had three married daughters and several grandchildren, all of whom lived in Williamson. She provided Carrie with their names and contact information.

Carrie called them; they could shed no light on why anyone would want to kill their mother, a caring woman who had lived simply, was devoted to her family and friends and committed to her church.

Chapter 68

Several days later, Annie was sitting at the desk in the gift shop while her managers, Martha and Patrick Kelly, took a lunch break. She was expecting Ed, who was bringing sandwiches and drinks for the two of them and for Jason, who was working upstairs in his office on press releases.

A few minutes past noon, Ed entered the building, chatting with two men who appeared to be in their 30s. After placing a paper sack of sandwiches and three bottles of iced tea on the desk, he greeted his wife. "Hi, Annie. I'd like you to meet Sean Graves and his husband, Max Mallory."

The two men were wearing cargo shorts, hiking boots and shirts rolled up at the sleeves. One carried a backpack; the other a camera.

The shorter, sandy-haired man put out his hand and shook Annie's hand. "I'm Max." Annie looked at his spouse, who was taller and dark-haired, and smiled. "Then you must be Sean." She shook his hand. "What can I do for you?"

Max responded, "Sean and I heard about this museum and wanted to meet you. We found something we think you might be interested in."

Ed, in the meantime, had retrieved two chairs from the board room. After sitting, the men proceeded to explain the purpose of their visit. Max had inherited an old cobblestone farmhouse on Port Bay that the couple had initially planned to demolish to construct a modern home as a vacation retreat.

"We live in Connecticut, but I commute to New York City where I'm the executive chef at a restaurant. Sean is a contractor which, given what we've decided to do with the property, is a real plus," Max volunteered.

Sean explained, "The house has been vacant for years, and we assumed it wouldn't be livable. We were surprised that it was in decent shape and decided to renovate it instead of tearing it down. I can do most of the work myself, with the help of subcontractors."

Max continued, "We fell in the love with the place. It's on the water, with acres of heirloom apple trees on the property. Some are diseased; we'll need to remove those; the others just need TLC and are still bearing fruit."

"We've been wanting a change in our lives," Sean added. "Max is tired of commuting to the city for a stressful job with unreasonably long hours, and I can do construction anywhere. We've decided to relocate here. We'll renovate the carriage house first and live in it while we renovate the main house, which we're going to turn into an inn with a small restaurant. We also want to start a cidery."

"That sounds like a wonderful life change," Annie enthusiastically responded, her eyes gleaming, "and the inn will be a positive addition to the community, but can I ask why you wanted to meet with me?"

The pair smiled. Sean stated, "Now that's where this gets interesting. We were rummaging around in the attic and found antiques, furniture and artwork that are in perfect condition and will be used to furnish the inn. We also found a diary. It's dated back to 1814, a man named Hiram VanEyck wrote it. Does his name mean anything to either of you?" He glanced at Ed and Annie, who looked at each other and shook their heads.

"He was a young, associate preacher who was apprenticing for Levi DeCleryk." Sean smiled.

"Oh, my, that's my ancestor," Ed exclaimed. "He and his wife Sarah were my great-grandparents several times removed. Although it makes sense that he would have hired an associate pastor to replace him when he retired, I've never heard of VanEyck."

"He died young, more about that later," Matt responded.

Sean continued, "We found the diary, thought it should be donated to an organization that would appreciate it, looked online and discovered this museum and that the executive director was a woman named Annie DeCleryk. We figured there had to be a familial connection."

Annie grinned. "As you've probably surmised, DeCleryk is my married name. I've been married to Ed for more than 40 years; I believe that by now some of his family's genes have filtered into my DNA." They all laughed.

"Tell us what's in the diary," Ed prompted.

"One of the things we learned," Matt responded, "was that Hiram was going to take over as pastor once Levi retired. The older man's health was failing, and he wanted to make sure he had a successor. In his early 20s, Hiram boarded with the DeCleryks but went home to visit his family as frequently as possible.

"He was engaged to a woman named Rowena Fallows, and once they got married, the plan was that she would move into the rectory of the church in Lighthouse Cove with him as pastor, and the DeCleryks would move into a smaller cottage nearby. Tragedy befell the couple before any of that happened. Rowena died of blood poisoning, and Hiram didn't live long enough to become pastor."

"That's why you're here, to tell me about the diary?" Annie asked.

Max held up his index finger. "Yes, partially, bear with me for a minute; this is where the story gets interesting. The villagers discovered that the British were on their way to Lighthouse Cove during the War of 1812, and to help protect it, Hiram joined a militia. A man named Robert Fitzhugh had organized it." Ed and Annie glanced at each other. Max continued, "Hiram died in battle, and he's buried here.

"His mother wrote a postscript at the end of the diary. It's a touching tribute to her son and she mentions where he was buried, what he was buried with and other details. We'd love to visit the cemetery and find his gravesite, if that's possible."

Max handed Annie the diary. "Of course, we want to donate this to the museum. It's in decent condition and should be displayed where others can view it."

Annie, pleased at their kindness, smiled and hugged both men. Then she handed the diary to Ed. "Maybe before we put this into an exhibit space, you'd like to read it, Ed. You might learn more about your family."

"I'll take it home with me and start reading it this afternoon," Ed promised.

Annie turned to the two young men. "Our cemetery was in terrible disrepair until lately. It's in the process of being restored, but we haven't yet placed any signs on the road to direct visitors to the site, and it's located in an out-of-the-way place in the woods. We can drive you there."

Ed looked concerned. "Are you sure you want to do that, Annie? I can take them by myself. You don't have to come with me if you're not ready."

"Yes, Ed, I do. I can't put it off forever." Turning to the young men, she explained that she had discovered the body of a dear friend who had been murdered at that cemetery several months ago.

"That's horrible," Sean responded.

"It is, but I'm going to have to go sometime. I'll be okay. Plus, I want to see what the garden club volunteers and the archaeologists we've hired have done with it."

After a short conversation, it was decided that Max and Sean would follow Ed and Annie, then stay and explore the cemetery, and the DeCleryks would return to the museum to eat their lunches. Annie called Jason on the intercom and asked that he join her downstairs. She handed him a sandwich and a drink, introduced him to Sean and Max, and explained that they were going to lead the men to the 1812 cemetery. She requested he remain in the gift shop until the Kellys returned, just in case they had visitors.

Jason walked to the door with them and watched as Annie and Ed got into their SUV and Max and Sean into a red truck. He shivered, uneasy. Seeing the truck reminded him of something, he just couldn't put his finger on what it was.

On the short drive to the cemetery, Annie had admitted to Ed that she was slightly apprehensive. After parking and escorting Matt and Sean to the site, she breathed a sigh of relief. The headstones had been repaired and replaced, pieces of bone and linen shrouds had been buried or discarded, clusters of flowers edged along bricked paths and around the burial sites, trees and shrubs had been pruned.

They walked along with the two young men, who peered at the stones looking for Hiram's grave. They found it, and Annie gasped. It was at the exact location where she and Suzanne had discovered George's body. His hand had been stretched out, touching Hiram VanEyck's burial mound.

Chapter 69

A fortuitous sequence of events resulted in solving the case. If Sean and Max hadn't visited the museum, if Jason hadn't been on the front porch to watch them leave with Annie and Ed, if Ed hadn't read Hiram VanEyck's diary and Annie hadn't joined the garden club and learned the names of the flowers that grew in parks and yards in the village, they'd probably still be puzzling over who killed their friend and Eleanor Brown, and the reason for Amanda's attack. Now they knew.

Ed and Annie left Sean and Max at the cemetery and drove back to the museum where they ate their sandwiches at a table on the front porch. Ed then went home to let Gretchen out and repaired to his study where he planned to spend the rest of the afternoon reading the diary. Martha and Patrick Kelly returned from lunch to work in the gift shop, Jason went back upstairs, and Annie went into her office to write her monthly report for the board of directors.

Something was nagging at her, something about the flowers that had been planted at the cemetery; she couldn't quite put her finger on why she was uneasy. Just as she remembered what was bothering her, Jason ran into her office.

"Annie, I remembered something from the day George Wright was murdered, something I didn't tell Ed or you about. At the time I didn't think it meant anything," he explained.

Dismayed, Annie confessed that she, too, had just remembered something. They were starting to put two and two together, and Annie didn't like the way the numbers were adding up. "This is upsetting, Jason. I need to call Ed. Why don't you stay with me and talk with him about your recollection of the sequence of events on that day."

She had just started to dial the number from her office phone when her cell phone rang. She picked it up and answered. It was Ed.

"Annie, I've finished reading the diary, and I believe I have the information I need to solve the case."

Chapter 70

An hour later, after a hasty meeting at the police station, Carrie, with Ed and Annie at her side, knocked on Amanda Reynolds' door. She answered within a few seconds, and her face lit up with a smile.

"What a lovely surprise, though I'm not sure why you're here. I'm hoping no one called to report that I'd been attacked again. As you can see, you have no reason to check up on me. Despite my advancing age and some physical infirmities, I'm perfectly fine." She chuckled.

"That's not why we're here, Amanda," Ed replied. "May we come in?"

Amanda opened the door and motioned that they follow her into the living room. "May I offer you some tea?" she asked, her voice sprightly.

Ed, noticing Annie and Carrie looking at him, shook his head. "No, thanks."

"I'm still going to brew some tea for myself," she countered and humming the hymn, *Glory, Glory Hallelujah*, went into the kitchen to put the kettle on.

Returning a few minutes later, she sat down, and slowly sipped her beverage. It smelled of herbs and spices, and a little like rice pudding. "Since you're not checking up on me, what is it that brings you here?" she asked calmly.

"We know who killed George Wright and Eleanor, Amanda, and we know the reason you were attacked," Ed responded.

"That's wonderful news, Ed. Have you arrested him? You must be relieved, and I certainly appreciate your letting me know. Now I won't have to lock my doors anymore." She laughed.

"George's killer was not a man," Ed replied, then looked at Annie. "You were absolutely on target when you suggested that poison is a woman's weapon of choice."

"Oh my! That's certainly shocking news. I can't believe a woman would be involved in committing such terrible crimes." Amanda shook her head, then clapped her hand to her mouth.

"It's Sally Wright, isn't it? I knew something was off about that woman when I met her at your party. She ordered a hit on her own husband and to take suspicion off herself made it look like his death had something to do with the War of 1812, didn't she? I thought a man attacked me, but I was wrong, wasn't I? It was her or someone she sent." She paused. "What I don't understand is why she would have killed dear Eleanor."

"Sally's not the murderer, Amanda." Ed replied.

Annie, livid, interrupted, "Amanda, please, stop the theatrics. I've seen you perform in summer stock enough times to know how talented you are. You're acting an Oscar-winning part here. You have been all along. You know exactly who the murderer is."

Her eyes opened wide and looking confused, Amanda responded, "I don't quite know what it is you're talking about, dear. I'm baffled that you would believe I know who killed George and Eleanor."

Ed was impatient and irritable. "Amanda, that's enough. I'll cut to the chase. You killed George and orchestrated your own attack, and we know why. What makes no sense is why you killed your friend, Eleanor."

"What are you talking about? Why on earth would I commit two murders? How can you even think that?" Amanda exclaimed.

Ed took the lead. "Jason Shipley walked to your house the day he visited you the first time, Amanda. As he approached it, you were standing at the door, waving to a man who was getting into a red truck. He was tall and lanky and had gray hair. That man was George Wright. You see, Annie had received a phone message from him, he'd found something at the cemetery that he wanted to show her.

"He sounded excited; he didn't say what he'd discovered, but now we know it was a watch with a message inside it. For some reason he knew about you and your reputation as an historian with expertise on the War of 1812 and not able to reach Annie, decided to show you what he'd discovered. He knew where you lived, and after retrieving his tools, he drove to your house on his way back to the cemetery. You knew immediately what the message meant, but by telling him you'd ruin your reputation. Instead, you poisoned him."

Amanda shrugged and shook her head. "That's preposterous."

Ed continued, "Two young men visited the museum earlier today. They found a diary written by a man named Hiram VanEyck. Hiram was part of the militia that your ancestor formed to repel the British invaders. As it turned out, Robert Fitzhugh was a traitor."

"Oh, Ed, that's just ridiculous!" Amanda scoffed.

"It's not. I read the diary. Hiram wrote that he discovered Fitzhugh's treachery after overhearing a conversation he'd had with a British soldier. A short while later, he confronted the man, and they fought. Fitzhugh pushed Hiram, who, trying to regain his balance to avoid falling, grabbed his attacker's jacket.

Fitzhugh's pocket watch fell off in the skirmish without him realizing it, then he ran to meet the British in order to escape.

"Hiram pocketed the watch, wrote a note with the words *RF-traitor* and placed it inside the back of the watch, which was engraved with Fitzhugh's initials and opened like a locket. He must have hoped if he died in the ensuing battle someone would discover it and his diary, which contained details that could prove his suspicions."

Ed continued, "Hiram's premonition was correct, he was killed during the British invasion, and although he would be interred in the cemetery for fallen heroes of that war, his family came to take him and his belongings, which included his diary and the watch, back to Port Bay to prepare his body for burial."

Amanda rolled her eyes and interrupted, "Are you saying you believe this? It sounds like a work of fiction, or at least the imaginings of a person with a deranged mind."

"Let me finish, Amanda. For an unexplained reason, instead of inscribing details of her son's internment in the family bible, which was traditional in those days, Hiram's mother wrote about them on the last page of his diary. She admitted the family had not read it, it would have caused them great pain to revisit his final days, and they didn't want to invade his privacy. That's probably why Fitzhugh's treachery was never discovered.

"His mother listed the items he was buried with, including the watch, a beautiful piece of cloisonné workmanship. She believed the initials on the back were those of his beloved fiancée, Rowena Fallows, who had died several months earlier.

"It appears that she never opened the back of it and didn't know about the message Hiram had written about

Fitzhugh being a traitor. Her description of the watch matches one that's been missing for centuries that should have been part of a permanent collection at the Victoria and Albert Museum. Annie showed photos of the collection to you and Eleanor after we returned from our trip to England. You professed surprise and shock; you were lying. We know you knew about it all along."

Chapter 71

Amanda's eyes closed for a second, then she opened them. She smiled like a cat who had not only caught a mouse but had eaten it alive, slowly and with relish.

"I guess there's no point to lying about it now," Amanda replied. "It appears the game is up. I confess I murdered George Wright. I had to do it. I had no choice; I couldn't let anyone know what happened, not after all the fame and glory I've received. My reputation would have been ruined. My book, for a time, was a best seller in greater Rochester, you know."

Annie was furious. She'd been duped long enough by this woman she'd once considered a friend, a woman she'd cared deeply about. She spoke up.

"You put foxglove in his tea, Amanda, which is essentially a weaker version of our modern-day drug, digitalis. A healthy person with no heart issues might become quite ill but most likely would survive, like you did when you administered it to yourself.

"What I don't understand is how you could have known that George had AFib and was on a beta blocker and that by giving him digitalis, he would die. What makes me even angrier is that you orchestrated your own attack to make it seem like the murderer was after both of you. It was a smoke screen to steer the investigation in another direction."

"How in the world did you figure it out?" Amanda asked.

Annie replied, "When I visited you a few weeks ago, you invited me to look at your garden. Since joining the garden club, I've become much better at identifying botanicals. I was pleased that I knew the names of all your beautiful flowers. I just didn't think anything about it at the time.

"Ed and I visited the cemetery earlier today, and I noticed clusters of foxglove plants at the site. I then remembered that among all the flowers in your yard you had planted foxglove, lily-of-the-valley, wolfsbane and larkspur, and then it hit me. Your garden was gorgeous but extremely lethal. I never would have realized it until I joined the club."

Amanda started to speak. Annie, exasperated, held up her hand. "Please, let me finish. On one of my other visits, you stayed on the back porch, and I said I'd let myself out. That was the day you came back into the house and saw me perusing the books on your bookshelves. One of the books was about medicinal and natural healing plants and herbs, and today I put two and two together."

Annie continued, "I can't imagine how you brewed the tea to make it taste good. I did some research and foxglove is supposed to taste bitter. The only possibility is that you must have masked it with something sweet.

"As we've confirmed, digitalis won't necessarily kill a healthy person. It can be deadly for someone with AFib, especially someone who is also taking a beta blocker. I know I'm repeating myself, but how could you possibly have learned about George's medical condition? Both you and Sally were at one of our parties this past spring, and I distinctly remember, after introducing the two of you, that you hugged her saying that while you'd never met George, you were sorry for her loss."

"Annie, I did know George," the older woman responded, now speaking more slowly. "You see, we both used the same medical practice, and one day several months ago we happened to be sitting next to each other in the waiting room and began to chat. I introduced myself and mentioned that I was an author, and we had a brief discussion about my book. Then he volunteered information about himself, that he was retired from both the Navy and being a financial adviser. We were pleased to learn we both lived in Lighthouse Cove, just a few blocks from each other.

"I asked him why he was there, and he explained that he suffered from AFib, took a beta blocker to control it and was having a follow-up that day to make sure the drug was working."

Carrie, who had been quiet for most of the discussion, looked at Amanda. "One thing puzzles me. You were certain that foxglove added to the tea combined with George's beta blocker would kill him. What would you have done if it hadn't?"

"Oh, there was no chance George would live." Amanda smiled. "You see, I've experimented with the combination before."

Chapter 72

Carrie, Annie and Ed stared at the woman, the enormity of her confession and what it portended dawning on them. Annie was the first to respond. "Oh, my. You killed someone else with the drug, didn't you?" She put her hand to her mouth.

"It was your husband, Ernest, wasn't it? I remember your telling me he had died in his 50s of heart failure, and at the time you didn't seem sad about it. You made a comment about his death being no great loss, and that bothered me.

"I assumed your marriage had been unhappy and that perhaps he had mistreated you. I felt sorry for you. I questioned you; you didn't seem to want to talk about it. I let it go, and then eventually forgot about it. He hadn't mistreated you and didn't die from natural causes, did he? You killed him."

"Ernest was a nasty, pesky man, and, yes, I killed him" Amanda sighed and closed her eyes for a few seconds. She seemed unfocused.

"Many years ago, we owned a small fishing cabin in Henderson Harbor. One Friday night after work, he went with a friend to the cabin for the weekend, they made a side trip to Sackets Harbor to have dinner that evening. He had wandered into a gift shop looking for a souvenir for me, came across the Morgan Lewis book and wanted to surprise me with it, believing I'd be delighted.

"I hadn't known it existed when I did the research for my own book. That night he read it and discovered that Fitzhugh was a traitor, and after he got home, he handed me the book and pointed out that I'd made many errors in my own book. Reporting that Robert Fitzhugh was a patriot had been a terrible mistake, and I was horrified, but for me there was no going back. I couldn't confess I'd not been thorough with my research; I simply couldn't risk the damage to my reputation.

"I was still teaching, and that Monday at lunch hour I called the gift shop in Sackets Harbor and ordered all their remaining copies. I made a mistake, and instead of having them sent to the school where I could have tossed them into a dumpster, I had them delivered to our home. After they arrived, I burned them in the yard. It was a boring book and not many copies had sold from reprints of the original. Other than me, few people alive today have read it.

"I must admit I was shocked when you showed up with the copy of the same book, Annie. I believed I had purchased all the remaining ones. I was relieved you'd not read it; if you had, you would have known that the premise of my book was based on a lie."

Impatient, Annie interrupted, trying to get Amanda back on track. "You confessed to killing your husband. Why? Did his death have something to do with the Morgan Lewis book?"

"I was getting to that, dear," Amanda responded, taking a deep breath, "Ernest came home that evening and smelled the smoke and asked what I'd done. He was quite displeased with my decision to destroy the copies and that I'd intended to pretend ignorance about Lewis' book and Fitzhugh's treachery. He urged me to go to my publisher with the truth. I couldn't do that. He insisted I had a moral and ethical obligation; I was obdurate.

"He was such a goody-two shoes, that man, and threatened to call my publisher himself. We had a terrible row about it. I didn't believe he'd follow through with his threat but couldn't be certain. If he spilled the beans, I knew I'd be a goner, my reputation would sink. I had to find a way to get rid of him. I needed peace in my life."

Amanda smiled. "And then I knew just what I'd do. He'd had high blood pressure for years, since he was in his 30s, and back then the gold standard for treating it was to prescribe a beta blocker. I did my research and discovered that a combination of that and digitalis could be lethal. That's about the time I started my herb and flower garden. His death was recorded as a heart attack, no one thought to conduct an autopsy. The poor man was under a lot of stress and had *had* blood pressure issues; no one questioned it."

"Your success at murdering Ernest without getting caught emboldened you, didn't it, Amanda? You were confident that you could deal with George in the same way. Could you please explain how he came to visit you that day?" Carrie asked.

Amanda rolled her eyes. "Oh, why not? I'll tell you, though, these questions are becoming tedious." She was breathing heavily and paused for a second to catch her breath.

She explained, "George had discovered the cemetery and found the watch that morning, then decided to start cleaning it up and went home to get tools and his truck. He'd called and left a message for you, Annie, but you never returned his call."

"I did return his call, Amanda, but unfortunately he was probably already dead."

"Whatever. Anyway, he was chomping at the bit to learn more about the watch and the message inside it.

He decided on his way back to stop by my house to show it to me, hoping I'd know something about it.

"Of course, I knew immediately what it was and what the message meant from reading Lewis' book, but I certainly wasn't going to be the one to tell him. I had to convince him to leave the watch with me. If he gave it to you, Annie, I knew you'd figure it out. I couldn't let him or anyone else broadcast to the world that Robert Fitzhugh was a traitor. I had to stop him.

"I knew he was eager to get back to the cemetery, but I convinced him to stay and join me for a cup of tea and a homemade scone, it would make an old lady's day. He agreed; he was a kind man, and remembering that he had AFib, I steeped black tea and foxglove leaves in a china pot for several minutes and then strained the beverage into his cup. He admitted he liked his tea sweet, which was fortunate for me. Annie, you were right, I needed to mask the bitter taste and added a liberal amount of honey. Then, before he left, I fixed a to-go cup for him. You may have noticed the bottles of medicinal tinctures in my kitchen? I made all of them from the plants in my garden. This time, I added ice and several drops of tincture of foxglove, just for insurance. He was appreciative; it would help hydrate him while he worked, he said. I also wrapped up the partially eaten scone."

Carrie asked, "How *did* you get him to let you keep the watch, Amanda?"

Amanda stood up and walked over to the sideboard, opened the bottom drawer, removed the watch and handed it to Annie. Her gait was slow, and her breathing had turned raspy.

Chapter 73

"I suggested that George leave the watch with me for safekeeping while he worked at the cemetery and promised I would begin doing research to check its provenance. He planned to collect it from me on his way home. He hoped, by then, I'd be able to find information about it, who it belonged to or what the message meant, and then he planned to hand it over to you, Annie.

"Of course, that was never going to happen. I knew that within moments after reaching the cemetery he'd be dead, and given its remote location in the woods, I expected no one would find him for several hours or maybe even days, despite his truck being parked on the road near the path. I just couldn't have my reputation sullied."

"It's likely no one would have found his body that afternoon, Amanda, if Suzanne Gordon and I hadn't hiked the path, looking for him," Annie replied. Then she remembered something else.

"The day I called and asked for the book back you lied to me. You said you'd spilled tea on it, but that's not true, is it?"

"No. I destroyed it. Just like I destroyed all the other copies I owned. Case closed."

Carrie spoke up. "I have a couple more questions, Amanda, before we Mirandize you and transport you to the station for booking. Why did you feel you had to implicate poor Francis Lewis in the murder? You must have known he was ill, and the trick you played on his wife and daughter was inexplicably cruel."

Amanda laughed gaily. "It was just too perfect an opportunity to overlook. I discovered a reproduction cloisonné watch online at a jewelry store in Wisconsin, and, of course, you know the rest of the story. I said we weren't related. I lied about that, too. Francis Lewis and I are cousins, and, yes, I was aware he's in declining health; a friend who lives in Oswego keeps me abreast of that family's status.

"Before Ernest died, we occasionally socialized with them. My husband enjoyed their company, but I never did, I thought Clarissa was so cold, and she seemed so superior. After Ernest was gone, I stopped responding to their invitations, and we lost contact. They probably don't even know I'm still alive."

Ed and Carrie shook their heads at the statement. Clarissa Lewis had seemed reserved, but she'd also been extremely loving and patient with her husband. There was nothing about her that indicated she felt superior to anyone.

"I had such fun preparing that note and putting a scare into them." Amanda continued, whispering conspiratorially, "And, of course, leading you on a wild goose chase."

"You can barely walk, and you can't drive. How did you get the note to the police station?"

"My dear, departed friend, Eleanor, drove me. We'd been out for the evening, church prayer group, then a late dinner and a nightcap at The Brewery. I asked Eleanor to swing by the police department on our way home, explaining that I wanted to drop off a thank-you note to Carrie for all the work she'd been doing to solve the crime.

"Eleanor, of course, had no idea what was in it. I kept it in my pocketbook and had no difficulty using my cane to walk over and put it in the mail slot, the office door was locked. She thought I was considerate to have written it."

"Yes, Eleanor was a dear and devoted friend, from all accounts," Carrie stated. "Why did you kill her?"

"She had to die so I could protect my secret. I'd invited her to join me for lunch one afternoon, chicken salad on croissant, and we were almost ready to eat. I asked that she go into the dining room to get place mats that were in the next to the last drawer of the sideboard. She was somewhat hard of hearing, and instead opened the last drawer and discovered the pocket watch. She thought it was beautiful and brought it into the kitchen to ask about it. I couldn't tell the truth so explained it was a family heirloom, and at first, she seemed to accept my explanation.

"Then, a few minutes later I caught her looking at me oddly. She must have remembered the day Annie showed us the photos of the exhibit in London and talked about a pocket watch that was missing from the collection. Eleanor seemed suspicious, and she certainly was a gossip. I feared she would say something about the watch to others, and I couldn't let that happen. She might have said something about it to you, Annie. You're smart, my dear, and I expect you would have realized that the watch was the one that was missing.

"I could do nothing about it that afternoon; lunch had already been prepared, and after I put the watch back in the drawer and retrieved the place mats, she never left my side. I couldn't let her live, there was way too much at stake, but killing her would have to wait.

"The story I told you about the night she died, it's mostly accurate except that instead of dropping me off after the movie, I invited her in for a nightcap. She loves that scotch-based liqueur that's infused with herbs and honey. I can't stand the stuff but kept it for her and spiked her drink that night with a generous amount of tinctures of foxglove, lily-of-the-valley and larkspur. Eleanor was healthy, and I knew the foxglove would have made her ill but wouldn't have been fatal. Fortunately, none of the poisons is terribly fast acting, she'd be home long before she became ill and died."

Her throat clogged with suppressed rage, Annie looked at Amanda, who was struggling for breath, and bitterly remarked, "And you admirably acted the part of the grieving and distraught friend. You missed your calling, you know, as a professional actress. You fooled all of us." Then, it hit her.

"Amanda, are you drinking foxglove tea? Did you just poison yourself?"

Amanda smiled a Mona Lisa smile. "Annie, I'm not going to go to jail for this, and I guess my time is up. My body's been failing me anyway, it's no fun not being able to walk without assistance or drive; leaving this earth earlier than I'd hoped is no great loss.

"No, it's not foxglove tea. The amount of foxglove in a cup of tea, as you learned, couldn't possibly kill me. I'm drinking wolfsbane tea spiked with a little of the larkspur; it has such a lovely smell, don't you think? And it's far more effective. You see, I knew the minute you all entered my house that you'd figured it out."

Carrie pulled out her phone and dialed 911. Amanda was dead before the EMTs reached the hospital.

Chapter 74

Ed, Annie, Jason and Carrie met several days later at the Bistro. Over cups of espresso (for Ed), decaf coffee with milk (for Carrie) and lattes for Annie and Jason, the group agreed that the murder would never have been solved without all pieces of the puzzle coming together on the same day. They acknowledged that the remaining piece, the unidentified tire tracks, were most likely those belonging to someone who had stopped earlier in the day to simply enjoy the view and had nothing to do with George's murder.

Annie remarked that while they had much to be thankful for, and that the Wright family was eternally grateful to them for finding George's killer, she didn't feel much like celebrating. She had considered Amanda a dear friend, and she couldn't shake off the weight of her betrayal. Jason confessed that he'd begun to care for the woman and couldn't understand how she had been warm and welcoming to him minutes after she had sent George back to the cemetery and to his death.

"She was a classic narcissistic sociopath, Jason," Ed replied. "They can be quite charming and are intelligent but also extremely convincing liars and can be quite manipulative. They understand how to show love, but they don't feel it. They have no remorse in doing what needs to be done to eliminate any perceived threat. I suspect Amanda believed she was superior to almost everyone she knew and that it was her right to do whatever she needed to maintain her skewed opinion of herself."

Jason shook his head. "She served me scones and tea and hugged me, even after the first time I met with her. How does someone who's a murderer do that?"

Carrie responded, "Don't be so hard on yourself, Jason. She was skilled at fooling all of us."

The scandal had made all the newspapers in upstate New York, including the dailies in Rochester, Syracuse and Buffalo, and to the group it seemed like Amanda's confession and subsequent demise was the only topic of conversation wherever they went.

Owners of local businesses, neighbors, friends, and even tourists were buzzing with comments and questions, and unanimously, they made a pact that should the topic came up again, they would politely respond that they no longer felt comfortable discussing it. They all wanted to move on with their lives.

Annie remembered again their summer brunch. Amanda had hugged Sally and pretended she hadn't known George. She couldn't fathom the level of depravity that caused the woman to kill three innocent and decent people and fake an attack to cast suspicion away from herself.

"I didn't know her at all; how could I have missed how diabolical she was?"

"Annie," Ed responded, taking her hand in his. "We were all misled, her church and garden club friends, her repertory theater group, neighbors, the members of the historical society."

Carrie added, "No one in Lighthouse Cove ever had a negative thought about Amanda, I can assure you. When you live in a small village you tend to trust those who are part of it, especially if they've been around for a long time. Amanda had been a pillar of this community; why would anyone in Lighthouse Cove believe anything ill about her?"

"I guess you're right, Carrie. Still, it's distressing. I'm puzzled about something else. After she discovered her own book wasn't factually correct, why didn't she just admit that new information had surfaced about her ancestor and that she would be rewriting parts of it?"

Ed answered, "Remember, she believed her reputation would have been ruined. She would never have been comfortable admitting her research wasn't thorough and she'd made mistakes."

"It ended up being her fatal flaw. At first her publisher might have been embarrassed and angry about publishing a book that was factually inaccurate," Annie responded, "but it's also possible Amanda would have been given a second chance to write the book as it was meant to be written. A new book might have sold even better than the first, especially with Robert Fitzhugh as the villain."

Carrie agreed. "Even if that hadn't happened, she may have been able to find another publisher. She was probably not the first author to have faced that sort of dilemma. I think most people would have applauded her for telling the truth." She sighed. "Truth, apparently, was not a word in Amanda's vocabulary."

A couple days later, after an emergency meeting of Annie's board of directors, she purged the library and gift shop of Amanda's books and papers. *The sad thing about it,* she thought to herself later, *was that the woman had been a talented writer, and within a few years no one will remember her accomplishments, nor will her legacy ever be a positive one. Now she'd be remembered as a liar and murderer.*

Chapter 75

The next several days would be busy ones. Suzanne and Garrett would be married that weekend and had decided to have their service on the grounds of the museum, with their reception held under a tent overlooking the water; weather permitting. In case of rain, they'd previously arranged to move the festivities to Peace Church.

For the wedding meal, the couple had chosen an eclectic menu to reflect Suzanne's Jamaican heritage and Garrett's, which was Puerto Rican on his mother side and Eastern European Jewish on his father's. Garrett had chosen his two sons as his attendants, Annie and Suzanne's two sisters-in-law would stand with her. *This celebration will take away the pain,* Annie reminded herself. *It's time to focus on something more positive.*

As it turned out, the wedding day dawned with a brilliant sun, clear sky and a perfect early fall temperature in the low 70s. Suzanne looked radiant in a simple ivory silk sheath with a single red hibiscus in her hair. Garrett, wearing cream-colored linen slacks and a navy silk shirt, grinned from ear-to-ear. His cognac-colored eyes gleamed as he watched his wife-to-be walk with her parents to the trellis, covered in white roses, where the pastor of the Unitarian Church that his parents attended would marry them.

Annie, who along with the other attendants stood on either side of the trellis, cried, and even Ed, who at times tried to be stoic, surreptitiously wiped his eyes.

The two enjoyed meeting Suzanne's and Garrett's families and reconnecting with his law partner, Sheila Caldwell, and her wife, Amy McBride, the pastry chef for Callaloo and baker of one of the most spectacular wedding cakes anyone had seen.

Chapter 76

A week later, Annie was sitting at her desk compiling the agenda for the next board meeting when her phone rang. It was Vincent Richards, Amanda Reynolds' attorney and executor of her estate. Annie groaned inwardly. She had no idea why he was calling and wasn't sure she was ready for a conversation with anyone who'd had an ongoing relationship with the murderer. The attorney was cordial and announced the reason for his call.

The Lighthouse Cove Museum and Historical Society had been named as one of the beneficiaries in Amanda's will, and the estate was substantial. Her cash investments were to be divided between the garden club and her church; she had willed her home and all its possessions to the museum.

Annie experienced a mixture of anger, sadness and joy. She scheduled a meeting with the attorney, requesting that Ed and Suzanne, now back from her wedding trip, join her for moral support. Two days later, they learned the full details of what Amanda had bequeathed to the organization.

Richards handed Annie the key to Amanda's house. "I know the circumstances of this are odd, and this must be difficult. In her own twisted way, she cared for you and wanted to make sure that Lighthouse Cove Museum benefitted from her estate. As you know, she had no children, and her only living relatives are scattered about; she'd had no contact with any of them for years. I'm hoping this helps you to heal and recognize that while what she did was appalling and horrific, inside that twisted mind was a person who at heart wanted what was best for the community. Maybe someday you'll find your way to forgiving her, or at least be able to move on and recognize the gift you are being given."

Annie's throat was clogged with emotion. Part of her wanted nothing to do with the inheritance; three innocent people had died because of an emotionally damaged woman. On the other hand, the historic home and its beautiful gardens would continue to be preserved and admired, and perhaps joy would emerge from tragedy.

From the Letters of Rebecca Fitzhugh

March, 1818
My dear sister,
    A year has passed since my previous letter. Much has transpired since that time that I've not been able to put into words until now. My sadness is without end, as I write to tell you that my beloved Robert has gone to his eternal rest and resides with our Lord Jesus.
    In penance for his role as a traitor in the War of 1812, he resolved to make our world a better place for all. Recognizing the immorality and cruelty of slavery, he became an abolitionist, although the movement in England is just beginning to gather steam. For many months, he had been working (yet, again undercover) to smuggle slaves out of England to Canada—where they may live as God intended—freely and without persecution or fear. Neither his father, mother nor the King knew of his plans and believed his frequent trips away from home to Canada were the result of business dealings. I swore to him that I would never betray his trust by informing them of his real mission.
    On his last trip, after he had successfully relocated three families of slaves to a small, free settlement in York, Upper Canada, British North America, he became quite ill with what we learned was the smallpox, the very disease that took our dear parents from us many years ago. The healers in the settlement, Thomas Battleforth, and his wife, who shares my name, Rebecca, worked tirelessly to save him, but to no avail. He died crying out for me and the children.

At times I feel I cannot bear this pain; it is too great. My three offspring resemble their well-favored father and carry his blood within them, and they are a constant reminder to me of the love he and I shared to the end. The girls grieve desperately; despite the emptiness they feel from his loss, they have settled comfortably in our adopted country, and Henry is thriving.

Robert's parents, who will forever believe that their son died on a trip to Canada to acquire new land holdings for his family, have implored me to continue to reside with them, assuring me that the children and I will always have a loving and comfortable home. I shall not return to New York; yet pray, should circumstances allow, that you and Remington will one day sail across the broad ocean, so I may view your countenance once again.

With much love,
Rebecca

EPILOGUE

Two days later, Suzanne, Ed and Annie entered Amanda's house. They hadn't been back since her death. The board was strongly considering turning the historic property into a museum, and in partnership with the garden club conduct guided tours of the house and gardens and offer the property for weddings and other special events.

For now, Annie determined to assess what was in the home that was worth keeping and what could be discarded. Much of the furniture was antique and in excellent condition; that would stay, along with the Persian rugs, silver and dishware. Amanda's clothing and cookware would be donated to her church for their rummage sale or to the local Salvation Army.

She walked over to the sideboard in the dining room, opened the top drawer and found nothing of interest or value in it or in the three drawers beneath it. She had sent the pocket watch back to England but hoped she'd find less valuable historical pieces that could be included with the museum's exhibit about the War of 1812.

Annie turned to her husband and friend, "Amanda claimed she wrote the book about her ancestor before knowing Fitzhugh was a traitor, and the revelation, after the fact, in Morgan Lewis' book, is why she murdered her husband, George and Eleanor. She couldn't bear the embarrassment or shame of people finding out her book was a sham.

"Maybe that's not true. Maybe, even before reading Morgan Lewis' book, she knew Fitzhugh had committed treason but decided that a romantic story about a hero had more caché and would sell better than one about a villain. We know Rebecca Fitzhugh wrote letters to her sister which supposedly have never been discovered, but what if Amanda had them all along and knew from the letters that Fitzhugh had committed treason? I have no idea how or where she would have come to possess them since she wasn't related to the sister; still, this is a small community, and anything is possible."

No one responded. Annie turned away, opened the last drawer, and after emptying most of its contents spied a package at the bottom wrapped in chamois. Her eyes widened. She motioned Ed and Suzanne over to view what she had discovered: inside the chamois was a collection of letters, secured with a velvet ribbon. Annie untied the ribbon. Like the pocket watch and Hiram VanEyck's diary, the letters written by Rebecca Fitzhugh to her sister were in almost perfect condition.

She shook her head. "She had them all the time. I wonder if what's in these letters will prove I'm right, that her book was a lie from the beginning. How horribly tragic and sad."

Ed put his hand on Annie's shoulder and kissed her cheek. "I think you're about to find out."

Deciding that she might want some privacy, Ed and Suzanne quietly took their leave, but not before Ed promised he'd cook dinner that night. It was the least he could do. She'd be greeted with a glass of wine, soft Johnny Mathis ballads playing on their sound system and a romantic slow dance before their meal. A gesture that would be Ed's way of demonstrating to his wife how much he appreciated her and the wonderful dance of life they shared together, a life, he later reflected, full of unwavering love, but one he knew could be fleeting.

Thanking them for their sensitivity, Annie, with the packet of Rebecca Fitzhugh's letters in hand, walked into the living room. Sitting in a wingback chair, she began to read. And there she stayed until she reached the end. Wiping her eyes, she thought, *what a shame Amanda couldn't understand that these letters, about deceit, imperfection and love, were much more compelling than the lies she told.*

Annie stood up, secured the letters with the ribbon, wrapped them in the chamois and with them in hand walked out the door, grateful that a warm dinner and a warmer husband would be waiting for her.

The End

ANNIE'S RECIPES

Salmon with Fennel and Tomatoes-Serves 4
1 ½ lb. salmon fillet
3 C. halved cherry tomatoes
1 medium fennel bulb, cored and thinly sliced
¼ tsp. salt
½ tsp. pepper
2 tsp. minced garlic
2 T. lemon juice
2 T. extra virgin olive oil
3 T. capers, drained and rinsed
1 ½ tsp. dried dill weed
1 T. Dijon mustard

Preheat oven to 400 degrees. Spray a large rimmed baking sheet with cooking spray. Rinse salmon and pat dry. Place salmon, tomatoes and fennel on pan and sprinkle with salt and pepper. In a small bowl stir together garlic, lemon juice, olive oil, capers, dill and mustard. Drizzle sauce over fish, tomatoes and fennel in pan and stir to coat. Roast 15-20 minutes or until salmon starts to flake.

Ellie's Calico Beans-Serves 12-16
1 lg. onion, chopped
6 slices bacon, chopped
1 clove garlic, minced
1 16 oz. can pork and beans in tomato sauce
1 16 oz. can lima beans, drained and rinsed
1 15 ½ oz. can red kidney beans, drained and rinsed
1 15 ½ oz. can butter beans, drained and rinsed
1 15 ½ oz. can garbanzo beans, drained and rinsed
¾ C. ketchup
1 C. molasses
¼ C. packed brown sugar

1 T. dry yellow mustard

1 T. Worcestershire sauce

Cook onion, bacon, garlic in skillet until onion is tender and bacon is crisp. Drain and place into a large bowl, adding remaining ingredients. Place in a 3 ½ to 4 qt. slow cooker and cook on low for 10-12 hours or on high for 4-5 hours. Can also be baked in a casserole in a 375-degree oven for one to two hours.

Tuna Nicoise-Serves 8

Salad

8 fresh tuna steaks about ½ lb. each

½ lb. fresh whole green beans, stems trimmed

1 lb. small baby potatoes

2 lbs. cherry tomatoes, halved

½ lb. Kalamata olives, pitted

8 hard-boiled eggs, peeled and cut in half (optional)

A bunch of Arugula

Dressing

3 - 4 T. white balsamic vinegar

1 tsp. Dijon mustard

¼ tsp. ground black pepper

10 T. extra virgin olive oil

Grill the tuna to desired level of doneness (rare to medium-rare works best). Steam beans and potatoes until cooked. Place Arugula on a large platter, then arrange the tuna, beans, potatoes, tomatoes, olives and eggs (if desired). In a small bowl, combine the vinegar, mustard and pepper until blended. Slowly whisk in the olive oil until emulsified. Drizzle dressing over fish and vegetables and reserve extra to pass separately.

Roasted Rosemary Lemon Chicken-Serves 4-6 with leftovers
   1 5-6 lb. roasting chicken
   Coarse salt
   Pepper
   2 large sprigs fresh rosemary (or a couple tablespoons of dried)
   1 large lemon, quartered,
   2 tsp. dried minced garlic
   1 large onion, thickly sliced
   Extra virgin olive oil
   1 C. chicken stock or white wine.

Preheat oven to 450 degrees, then lower to 375 degrees after 15 minutes.

Remove chicken giblets. Rinse chicken inside and out, remove excess fat and pinfeathers and pat the outside dry. Put sliced onion in the bottom of the roasting pan and place chicken on top. Salt and pepper inside of the chicken and stuff the cavity with the garlic, lemon quarters and one spring of rosemary. Pour olive oil over top of chicken and crumble second spring of rosemary on top along with more salt and pepper, if desired. Tie legs together and tuck wing tips under body of chicken. Pour broth or wine into the pan. Roast chicken for 15 minutes, uncovered, then lower oven temperature to 375 degrees. Baste every 15 minutes with pan juices (add more wine or broth if necessary) until temperature at the breast is between 165-170 degrees (about 15-20 minute per pound). Remove chicken from oven, let sit for 20 minutes before carving.

Green Bean and Potato Salad-Serves 10-12
2 lbs. mixed color fingerling potatoes
1 lb. green beans, trimmed
¼-1/2 C. mixed fresh herbs
2 T. extra virgin olive oil
½ tsp. freshly grated lemon zest.
Salt and pepper

In a large pot, simmer potatoes in salted water to
cover until tender, about 8-10 minutes. Drain in a large
colander. In another pot cook beans in salted water until
crisp tender, about 3-5 minutes, until they turn bright
green. Drain into the colander with potatoes. In a large
bowl, toss the potatoes and beans with the remaining
ingredients. Add salt and pepper to taste. May be
refrigerated for a day or can be served warm or at room
temperature.

Annie's Gazpacho-Serves 8-10
Two unpeeled cucumbers, seeded and cut into
chunks
Two red peppers, cored and seeded
4-6 plum or other meaty, ripe tomatoes
1-2 large red onions
4 minced garlic cloves
6 cups tomato juice
½ C. white wine, red wine or cider vinegar
½ C. extra virgin olive oil
1 T. coarse salt
1 t. ground black pepper.

In a food processor with a chopping blade,
separately chop the cucumbers, peppers, tomatoes and
onion and place in a large bowl. Keep pieces chunky
and don't over process. Add the remaining ingredients,
mix together and chill. Will keep for a couple weeks or

more if stored in refrigerator in a large pitcher with a closed top.

Chinese Chicken Salad-Serves 6-8
<u>Salad</u>
1 pre-roasted chicken cut into pieces or strips or three or four packages or roasted or grilled chicken strips

1 bunch asparagus (about a pound), ends trimmed, blanched or microwaved until crisp tender and cut into thirds diagonally

2 red bell peppers, cored and seeded and cut into strips

A bunch of scallions, white and green parts, sliced

2 T. white sesame seeds toasted (can purchase pre-toasted or "toast" in microwave for a minute or so until they become golden brown

<u>Dressing</u>
1 C. vegetable oil (I use canola)
¼ C. apple cider vinegar
1/3 C. soy sauce
3 T. dark sesame oil
1T. honey
2 garlic cloves, minced
½ tsp. dried ginger
1 T. toasted white sesame seeds
½ C. smooth peanut butter
Salt and pepper to taste.

Combine shredded chicken, asparagus, and peppers in a large bowl (can use snow peas instead of or in addition to asparagus). Whisk all the ingredients together for the dressing and pour over the chicken and vegetables. Add scallions and sesame seeds and season to taste. Serve cold or at room temperature.

Provencal Sandwiches with Tuna, Basil and Tomato-Serves 6-8

½ C. red wine vinegar
6 flat anchovy fillets, rinsed, patted dry and minced
2 garlic cloves, minced
2 8-inch round loaves crusty bread
2 C. sliced radishes
2 C. loosely packed basil leaves
1 C. minced onion, soaked in cold water for 10 minutes and drained
1 6 ½ oz. cans tuna, drained and flaked
4 vine ripened tomatoes, sliced thin

In bowl whisk vinegar, anchovies, garlic, salt and pepper to taste. Add oil in a stream, whisking until emulsified. Half breads horizontally and hollow out halves, leavening ½-inch thick shells. Spoon one fourth dressing evenly in each half.

Working with one loaf at a time, arrange half the radishes and top with ¼ basil in the bottom of shell. Sprinkle half the onion over basil. Arrange half the tuna on onion and top with one-third remaining basil. Arrange half the tomatoes on basil and fit top shell over tomatoes. Repeat with second loaf. Wrap sandwiches in plastic wrap and put in a shallow baking pan. Top sandwiches with a baking sheet and a large bowl filled with weights (You can also put something heavy on the baking sheet- purpose is to compress the bread). Chill at least one hour, but sandwiches may be made 4-6 hours ahead, chilled and covered. Cut into wedges to serve.

Pasta with Pesto, Peas and Pine Nuts-Serves 12-15
1 lb. fusilli pasta
1 lb. ziti or penne
¼ C. extra virgin olive oil
1 ½ C. store-bought pesto
1 10 oz. package frozen, chopped spinach, defrosted and squeezed dry
3 T. freshly squeezed lemon juice
1 C. mayonnaise
½ C. shredded Parmesan cheese
1 ½ C. frozen peas, defrosted
½ C. toasted pignolia nuts
Salt and pepper to taste

Cook pastas separately according to directions for al dente. Drain and toss with olive oil. Cool to room temperature. In the bowl of a food processor with a chopping blade, puree the pesto, spinach and lemon juice. Add mayonnaise and puree until fully blended and thick. Add cheese. Add mixture to pasta, then add the peas, pignolias and salt and pepper. Mix together and serve at room temperature.

Lemon Tart with Blueberries and Raspberries-Serves 8-10
1 pie shell (can make from scratch or use store-bought) for a 9-inch pie plate
1 ½ jars lemon curd
1 pint each, blueberries and raspberries

Cook the pie shell according to directions. Cool completely. Spoon lemon curd into pie shell to cover bottom completely. Sprinkle blueberries and raspberries on top of lemon curd (or use one of the fruits). Cover with plastic wrap and refrigerate.

ABOUT THE AUTHOR

Karen Shughart studied English Literature at S.U.N.Y Buffalo, received a B.A. in Comprehensive Literature from the University of Pittsburgh and completed graduate courses in English from Shippensburg University.

She is the author of two non-fiction books and has worked as an editor, publicist, photographer, journalist, teacher and non-profit executive. *Murder in the Cemetery: An Edmund DeCleryk Mystery,* is the second in the series featuring the retired police chief and his intrepid wife, Annie. The first in the series is *Murder at the Museum.*

Before moving to a small village on the southern shore of Lake Ontario, Karen and her husband resided in south central Pennsylvania, near Harrisburg. To sign up for her blogs and newsletters or for more information, visit her website at www.karenshughart.com.